Praise for *Dying to Be Thin*

"More fun than an exploding Whoopie Pie! When plus-sized and out-of-work news producer Kate Gallagher heads for Durham, North Carolina, the 'Diet Capital of the World,' to take up residence at a diet clinic, she finds more than low-cal meals and fellow dieters. Instead, the plucky heroine is introduced to a dead diet doctor with a love for S and M, dueling diet clinics, and more suspects than she can shake a carrot stick at, not to mention a charming detective who finds Kate delightfully delicious."

—Sue Ann Jaffarian, author of *Booby Trap*

"A delightful debut. Plus-sized TV producer Kate Gallagher is as irresistible as a pint of mocha chip ice cream—without the guilt."

—Susan Kandel, author of *Christietown*

"Dishes out generous servings of humor and whodunit. . . . Fun and fast-paced, this quirky cozy truly puts the *die* into *diet*."   —Susan McBride, author of the Debutante Dropout Mysteries

"*Dying to Be Thin* made me laugh so hard, I choked on my M&M's. They say comedy comes from pain, and anyone who has tried to lose that pesky last fifty pounds knows how painful that can be. When spunky, chunky Kate takes on a murder investigation while trying to take off weight, the result is sheer delight. Kate Gallagher is the funniest, most adorable heroine in recent memory. Bridget Jones, eat your heart out!"

—Pamela Eells, executive producer of *The Suite Life of Zack and Cody*

"Ms. Lilley has crafted a humorous story and blended in a delightful cast of characters."

—The Romance Readers Connection

"Kate Gallagher is quirky, witty, and tough when she needs to be. She can also ferret out information better than a homeland security interrogator." —Pop Syndicate

Also by Kathryn Lilley

Dying to Be Thin
A Killer Workout

MAKEOVERS CAN BE MURDER

A Fat City Mystery

Kathryn Lilley

AN OBSIDIAN MYSTERY

OBSIDIAN
Published by New American Library, a division of
Penguin Group (USA) Inc., 375 Hudson Street,
New York, New York 10014, USA
Penguin Group (Canada), 90 Eglinton Avenue East, Suite 700, Toronto,
Ontario M4P 2Y3, Canada (a division of Pearson Penguin Canada Inc.)
Penguin Books Ltd., 80 Strand, London WC2R 0RL, England
Penguin Ireland, 25 St. Stephen's Green, Dublin 2,
Ireland (a division of Penguin Books Ltd.)
Penguin Group (Australia), 250 Camberwell Road, Camberwell, Victoria 3124,
Australia (a division of Pearson Australia Group Pty. Ltd.)
Penguin Books India Pvt. Ltd., 11 Community Centre, Panchsheel Park,
New Delhi - 110 017, India
Penguin Group (NZ), 67 Apollo Drive, Rosedale, North Shore 0632,
New Zealand (a division of Pearson New Zealand Ltd.)
Penguin Books (South Africa) (Pty.) Ltd., 24 Sturdee Avenue,
Rosebank, Johannesburg 2196, South Africa

Penguin Books Ltd., Registered Offices:
80 Strand, London WC2R 0RL, England

First published by Obsidian, an imprint of New American Library,
a division of Penguin Group (USA) Inc.

First Printing, September 2009
10 9 8 7 6 5 4 3 2 1

This book is dedicated to my husband, Gene, with love

Chapter 1

Murder's never perfect.

—Billy Wilder

Everyone wants a body to die for.

Especially me. My name is Kate Gallagher, and I'm a perfect size sixteen, which is an *un*perfect size for someone in my line of work. I'm a reporter in TV news—a field where any female bigger than a size two is practically an endangered species. Zaftig gals like me are vulnerable members of the newsroom herd, so I have to spend much of my time beating off the News Barbies, who are constantly on the prowl for my job. In broadcasting, the law of the jungle is up or out, but for mostly cosmetic reasons (174 of them, last time I checked in with the scale), my career has stalled in my adopted hometown of Durham, North Carolina. For me the town might as well be called Fat City.

My body/career problems came to a head last summer when I was summoned to Beatty the

Beast's office. Beatty is the news director at Channel Twelve Action! News. His favorite sport is torturing reporters with asinine assignments designed to jack up the station's perpetually sagging ratings.

Monday morning started off with a bang that week when Beatty eyed me across his desk and announced that he had a brilliant idea for an investigative series.

"Quick-weight-loss scams—they're a billion-dollar business." Beatty paused for dramatic effect. "What are they? Who suffers? Who's ripping off Thunder Thighs?"

He lobbed a glance at my hip zone and added, "I want *you* on the fat-scam story, Gallagher. You know the territory."

I shifted in my skintight wiggle skirt, which I'd bought fifteen pounds ago. Too many drive-through dinners and no-show sessions at the gym had left me and my skirt with more waddle than wiggle.

"Well, I've heard of a place where they *claim* to melt off cellulite," I said. "First they slather you all over with some kind of cream; then they wrap you up in plastic and stick you in a sauna. It's just water loss, though—totally bogus."

"Fantabulous. That's a dynamite visual." Beatty raised his fingers in the air and twisted a pair of phantom knobs. "I see you doing the story in a bikini. You're being frosted with fat cream and shrink-wrapped."

I blanched. "A *bikini*?" I said. "No way. I don't even own a bikini."

"You can expense it. We've got to see them slathering you in the cream, so that means bikini. The rest is up to you. I want a five-part series on diet scams for sweeps week."

When I didn't reply, his eyebrows shot up above the rim line of his aviator glasses, hairy protuberances that usually represented the leading edge of an ass-kicking squall.

"Investigative stories are *your* beat, Gallagher," he said. "But if you can't handle this one, I'll put Lainey on it. She's itching to do a series. And I'm sure she'd have no problem wearing a bikini."

"Lainey would prance naked on a catwalk if it meant promoting herself," I said.

Beatty yanked off his glasses and tossed them on the desk. "In case you forgot, Gallagher, this station's ratings pay your salary, so spare me any yada yada about how you won the duPont Award and you only do 'serious' news. We could use more people around here with Lainey's attitude."

Ouch. Lainey Lanston was my newsroom rival and personal nemesis. Formerly a print reporter at the *Durham Ledger*, she had always dismissed

TV news as lamebrain puffery—until the morning she showed up for her first day of work at Channel Twelve. Ever since then she'd been breathing down my neck, trying to outscore me on getting lead stories. The fact that Beatty was calling Lainey by her first name meant she'd already oozed her way into his good graces. A bad omen for me.

I gritted my teeth and said, "Lainey's completely wrong for this story—I already have some good sources. I'll do it."

When his eyebrows remained aloft, I added grudgingly, "Okay, including the damned visual with the bikini."

"Atta girl." Beatty flashed some teeth in a smile that might have been meant to be conciliatory. "And give me your usual hard-hitting stuff," he said. "Not like that piece of crap we ran yesterday about the escaped zoo tiger. We promote it as a killer, but then we show it holed up in a bush having kittens."

"Cubs. Tigers don't have kittens."

"Whatever." Another gesture dismissed me. "They were milk-eaters, not man-eaters."

"All you had to do was play up the happy-ending twist. That would've worked."

"Hey, that woulda been fantabulous," he said with another show of canines. "Maybe I should move you over to features."

"Maybe it's time for me to leave."

I fled from Beatty's office and cut a path through the crowded newsroom, avoiding the curious stares of my colleagues. I knew they were dying to pump me for information about my closed-door session with the news director, so I took refuge in an editing booth.

I opened my cell phone and called Evelyn, a former desperate housewife turned delighted divorcée. Evelyn was my friend and go-to gal for the latest scoop on fighting flab—we'd met a couple of years back when we were both on a wacky fruit diet at one of Durham's residential diet clinics (aka fat farms). But unlike me, Evelyn had kept all of her weight off, and then some. She picked up on the second ring.

"*Oh* my God, I can barely talk." Evelyn's voice sounded agonized. "I'm dying my pubie hairs Sunset Blond. This stuff stings like a holy mother."

"I think you're supposed to use a special hair dye for that," I said. "Without bleach."

"Ugh. No wonder. I'll just shave everything off."

"Good idea. Why did you want to go blond down south?"

"To make the carpet match the drapes, silly," she replied. "Tonight's the big night with Liam—everything's got to be perfect."

Perfection is Evelyn's holy grail when it comes to her body. She has her plastic surgeon on speed dial.

Over the sound of water being turned on, she continued, "Liam's coming over tonight to help me road test my brand-new breasts. With these D-cup babies he'll think he died and woke up inside a centerfold," she said. "And hopefully he won't feel the staples—I just had the surgery a month ago. Are you at work?"

"Yes, and I have a huge problem," I replied. "My news director wants me to wear a bikini on the air for some stupid series about weight-loss scams. Can you imagine me baring this jelly belly on TV? Right now I can't even zip up my thin jeans. Seriously—I've reached critical ass."

Evelyn made a soothing noise. "Hon, you've got a fabulous hourglass shape," she said. "And that gorgeous face of yours makes everyone jealous, *including* me."

My brain autorejected her compliment, partly because Evelyn has a much more forgiving attitude about her friends' bodies than about her own. But it was more than that.

You have such a pretty face was a refrain I'd heard ever since I was an adolescent—right before I heard *Now, if you could just lose some weight . . .*

The net result was that I'd wound up thinking

that having a pretty face served only to draw attention to the flaws everyplace else. Like my hips.

"I only have an hourglass shape when I'm wearing my waist cincher," I moaned. "And I can't wear a cincher with a two-piece."

"If you're really worried, just go see Dr. Medina," Evelyn said. "He's one of the primo guys in the entire Southeast. Seriously—he did an awesome job on my breasts."

"You mean lipo? Plastic surgery?" A little quacking noise escaped from my throat. "Yikes. That's way too drastic."

"But this isn't surgery. Dr. Medina has a new thermo-laser thingee that melts away the fat. It tightens your skin, too. And it takes only an hour—you can do it over lunch."

"I don't know, it sounds—"

Before I could say that Dr. Medina's "thermo-laser thingee" sounded like one of the fat-loss scams I was supposed to be reporting about, Evelyn steamrollered ahead. "Kate, this is actually a golden opportunity," she said. "You know how I've been pestering you to come to my body-image group?"

"Uh, body-image group?" I said, as if she hadn't mentioned the subject a thousand times before. "What's it called again? The Nudiebods?"

"The Newbodies. All the women there are *rav-*

ing about Dr. Medina's lunchtime lifts. Come with me to our meeting tomorrow night."

When I hesitated, she added in a firm tone, "No thinking! Anyone who has to wear a bikini on camera needs all the support she can get."

I couldn't argue her point. And besides, what did I have to lose by going to the support meeting? At the very least I might be able to develop some leads about fat scams for my series.

"Support group" didn't come close to describing the Tuesday night meeting of the Newbodies; the weekly get-together was more like a tribal gathering, a ritual that involved much venting around the fire pit and the imbibing of copious amounts of spirit juice. It was fabulous.

"All of the women here are going through one of the four cycles of love," Evelyn whispered in my ear. "Breaking up, losing weight, having plastic surgery, or starting a new relationship."

At least I didn't have to worry about the breakup part of the love cycle. I had an adorable boyfriend, Jonathan Reed, who was a homicide detective on the Durham PD. Okay, maybe he *was* missing in action at the moment, but that was only because he was in the UK visiting his sick mother. He'd be back in a couple of days.

Evelyn adjusted the sparkly center jewel on her plunging Sky top. The four of us—Evelyn and I, and Evelyn's new boobs—were perched on a settee in Trish Putnam's living room. The women of the Newbodies were arranged in a semicircle at our feet, sprawled on scattered stacks of fringed floor pillows. Trish—a high-voltage blonde whose expression seemed permanently shocked into wide-eyed surprise—claimed that pillows were more emo than chairs. But they looked uncomfortable to me, so I was grateful that Evelyn had staked out the settee.

"Kate, I'm *so* glad you came tonight," Trish said to me. "Evelyn told me you're having a body-image crisis."

Thrusting a platter of brownish blobs under my nose, she added, "Don't worry about these oat drops—they have negative points on Weight Watchers. The more you eat, the more you lose."

"Thanks. Good to know." I bit into an oat drop, which tasted like it had dropped from the end of a horse.

We went around the room to introduce ourselves and describe our body challenges. When it was my turn, I said, "Well, I have to wear a swimsuit for a news story. A bikini, actually. The entire Triangle viewing area is about to get a close-up view of my ab flab on the six o'clock news."

My announcement caused everyone to shift back on their pasha pillows in horrified silence.

Trish recovered first. "Things could be worse!" she exclaimed. "If you were on the network news, you might wind up on the front page of the *National Enquirer*. Did you *see* what they did to Kirstie Alley?"

This set off a round of nods, which quickly volleyed into spirited endorsements of Dr. Medina's cellulite remedies, including his lunchtime laser lifts.

"Dr. Medina's a miracle worker," Evelyn proclaimed. "If you don't believe me, just get a gander at *these*!"

With a dramatic flourish, she ripped off her Sky top, something she'd obviously been itching to do ever since we'd arrived. There was no bra underneath.

Freed of their netting, her breasts buoyed upward, revealing a pair of perfectly dimpled areolas and nipples the size and color of toasted minimarshmallows. Evelyn's chest was living proof that the laws of gravity had been defeated by the Age of Plastic.

Evelyn's Big Reveal was met by squeals and a round of applause. When Trish jumped to her feet and joined her in a bump and grind, the room exploded with a cacophony of jungle calls and pant-hooting. Trish must have been right about the pillows turning the emo on. We were chimp-chicks gone wild.

My nose caught a faint whiff of something sweet and thick smelling, like burned sage. It was marijuana smoke.

I turned my head. A shaggy twentysomething guy in a rumpled flannel shirt had appeared quietly behind me near the perimeter of the room. Looking a bit like a giant sheepdog, he was watching Evelyn's floor show with intense concentration. His pupils were dilated—from smoking weed, no doubt—and his hands were clutching a handheld gaming device. Perhaps in his altered state he thought Evelyn was a 3-D projection of a groovy chick from his video game.

"Chaz!"

Trish made a swooping dive at the kid. "Get back to your room right now, Chaz Putnam!"

As the hapless Chaz retreated down a hallway, Trish scolded, "I told you before—the entire front of this house is reserved for women only tonight. Don't you dare come back out here until after ten o'clock. At *least*."

"Bye, Chaz." Using both her hands, Evelyn blew him a Betty Boop–style kiss. She didn't seem the least bit embarrassed that he'd seen her topless.

"Don't encourage him, Evelyn," Trish said with a roll of her eyes. "Ever since he dropped out of grad school, Chaz has been creeping around the house like some kind of depressed rodent.

All he does is play on those computers, day and night. I don't know how many he has up there in his room right now. Our power bills have been unbelievable since he got home. I'd make him move out except he pays all his bills, and then some."

I would have added *stoner* to Trish's collection of loser nouns for her son.

I felt a light slap on my shoulder.

"Hey," a voice said. "Where've you been, stranger?"

Jana Miller had commandeered Evelyn's spot next to me on the settee. She must have snuck in during the Chaz rousting.

I gave Jana a huge hug. "*You're* the one who abandoned ship, you rat!" I said, raising my voice to be heard over the commotion.

I hadn't seen Jana in almost two years. In her mid-forties, Jana was a fellow veteran of the Fruit Diet clinic, where she'd shed an incredible amount of weight—more than a hundred pounds. The instant she reached her goal, she'd gotten a quickie divorce and an even quickier remarriage. Then she and her new husband had moved to Florida.

Jana radiated with a Miami glow from her strappy metallic sandals and purse to her page-cut hair, which was shot through with streaks of tricolor gold.

"I'm only in town for a couple of days for a consultation with Dr. Medina," she said. "He took off some excess skin back when I lost my weight on the Fruit Diet. But now I think I need a torsoplasty."

When I looked puzzled, she added, "A tummy tuck. Time for another tune-up. God. I must've spent fifty thousand dollars in the past couple of years on surgeries, easy pie."

"Oh," I said. "Well, you certainly look ten years younger. Do we credit Dr. Medina for that, or is it married love?"

Jana's glow lost some of its wattage. "It's just Dr. Medina's magic, I'm afraid."

Uh-oh. Things must not be working out with her new husband. I wanted to kick myself for bringing up the topic.

Before I could dig myself any deeper, Jana said, "I'm actually on my way to have dinner right now with my daughter, Shaina," she said. "It's our first reunion in two years. She was so upset when I married Gavin that she boycotted the wedding and took off to do volunteer work in Belize. She just flew in to Durham today to meet me."

Jana's daughter wasn't the only one who hadn't liked her mother's choice of second husband. Gavin was a self-proclaimed investor of "independent means," which was widely rumored to be no means at all. Jana, on the other hand, came from an old Louisiana family that had converted its diminishing old money into a new-money fortune by developing a cell phone franchise. Most of her friends—me included—suspected that Gavin had married Jana for her money.

Leaning in, Jana said, "Listen, Kate, I only stopped by tonight because I heard you'd be here," she said. "Can we get together for lunch this week? There's something I'd like to talk to you about."

"Sure," I said, reaching for my purse. "Let me check my calendar."

"Actually, it's kind of urgent. Would tomorrow be okay? I hate to put you out."

"No problem. Tomorrow's fine."

The expression on her face made me add, "Are you sure you don't want to talk right now, Jana? We could go outside or find a quiet room."

But Jana was already jumping to her feet. "No, I've got to go meet Shaina or I'll be late," she said with a distracted look on her face. "So tomorrow is really okay for you? How about Becca's Bistro?"

"That'd be great," I said, trying to cheer her up with a grin. "I love Becca's. I used to fantasize about their desserts all the time when we were starving on the Fruit Diet."

"Me, too." Jana responded with a smile, but it didn't touch her eyes. "Thank you so much, Kate. See you tomorrow."

Without saying a word to anyone else, she headed for the door.

Chapter 2

"Help, Evelyn! My ass is being attacked by giant daisies," I announced the next morning, smacking my butt for effect.

"It can't be that bad," Evelyn called from the other side of the dressing room door. We were shopping at a bathing-suit store called Swimsuit Heaven. But after sweating through a series of god-awful try-ons, I felt like I was burning in Swimsuit Hell.

Evelyn poked her head inside and squinted at my latest candidate, which paired a bandeau top with a pair of flower-power bikini bottoms. "Uh, right. That one not so much," she said.

"This is totally hopeless. Maybe I can attach some superlong hair extensions and hide my body underneath them to do the story. It worked for Lady Godiva," I replied. "The viewers will just think I'm naked."

The reflection of my bare belly under the fluorescent dressing-room lights was worse than I'd feared. When my waist cincher was removed, it had unleashed a short stack of bulges that spread east and west. To make things worse, each roll of fat was stippled with a line of bite marks where the cincher's hooks had once held it in check.

"I can't do this." I shook my head violently. "I can*not* go on camera with this body. I'll quit my job first. That's what I'll do—I'm gonna quit."

A young-sounding voice trilled through the latticed door, "How are we *doing* in there?"

"We're doing peachy as frickin' hell in here, thanks," I snapped.

A teenaged salesgirl peered past Evelyn, who was still standing in the doorway. Her eyes widened as they registered the imprinted row of dark pink hook marks on my newly unbound flesh.

"Oh, I'm so sorry—I didn't know you just had stomach surgery," the girl whispered, and quickly retreated.

As I scowled and squirmed my way out of the bandeau top, Evelyn placed her fists on her hips. "You're not even going to *think* about quitting your job," she said. "And may I point out the obvious? Jonathan loves every inch of your body. I can tell by the way he looks at you."

"Well, get this—he's never seen me naked with the lights on."

Evelyn stared at me. "Are you serious?"

Since her divorce, Evelyn had memorized every episode of *Sex and the City*. She must have assumed that was the way *all* singletons had sex.

"It's not that unusual." I tried to keep a defensive note from creeping into my tone. "I always set a romantic mood by putting on an outfit I buy online from Sexy Divas. Then, when things heat up, I turn off the lights. He thinks I do that because I was raised Irish Catholic. Oh God." I grabbed hold of both sides of my hair as a new thought whapped into my brain.

"What? *What?*"

"Jonathan's squad mates are going to see this series," I said. "Every cop in town is going to see more of me naked than *he* has. Oh, shit."

I leaned my back against the mirror, then slid

slowly down into a sitting position on the floor, legs splayed out in front of me. The sudden compression squeezed out my stomach below the belly button like a water balloon.

"I'll be humiliated," I moaned. "*He'll* be humiliated. He'll break up with me."

"No, he won't—stop it. Just share your feelings with him when he gets back from the UK." Evelyn was into sharing feelings in a major way. She touted it as a cure-all that could bring about world peace.

When I didn't respond, she added, "When's Jonathan due back?"

"Next week, I think."

"You *think*?"

"Well, he didn't exactly tell me."

"Oh?" Evelyn glanced away. "Huh."

"What huh?"

When she didn't answer, I glared at her until finally she shrugged. "Well, whenever a guy doesn't *exactly* tell me what's going on, I kick his planet's butt right out of my solar system," she said.

"Well, give him a break, Judy Jetson. His mother had pneumonia, for Pete's sake."

"Sorry about that, but it doesn't make any difference," she replied with a sniff. "Guys are like dogs—you have to teach 'em how to heel."

"Maybe with some men you do, but not with Jonathan."

I didn't want to tell Evelyn that there'd been some tension between Jonathan and me just before he'd left for the airport. It had been over something completely stupid, something that was sure to blow away as soon as we talked again, but still. Right then I was a little bit worried.

Evelyn snapped her wrist like someone jerking back on a leash. "All I know is, it never hurts to give 'em a little yank every now and then," she said. "Especially with a guy as hot as he is."

I thumped my head against the mirror and squeezed my eyes shut. "You're right—he *is* hot," I said. "So why would he want to see me naked? *I* don't even want to see me naked. Clearly my love life is over."

"No, it isn't," Evelyn countered. "You just have to have some faith in yourself—and in him."

When I refused to open my eyes, she added nervously, "I'll go find some tanning cream. It does miracles for minimizing." She bolted from the dressing room.

Make him heel. I'd never dream of playing manipulative games like that with Jonathan. But here was a harsh countertruth: Only women who have great bodies *could* play those games. I wasn't even qualified to step onto the field.

I'd observed plenty, though. For example, I'd noticed that whenever Jonathan and I were out together, the women who entered his radius warmed to his British accent and blue-green eyes, which ignited whenever a smile cracked through his homicide cop's reserve.

Jonathan had never given me any cause to suspect that he paid attention to come-hither signals from other women. But then why had he stopped calling me daily from the UK? Something bad was obviously going on. Maybe his mom had gotten worse.

Or maybe the problem was with me. Jonathan had looked baffled—and a little pissed—right before he left for the UK, when I'd refused for the umpteenth time to let him join me in my morning shower. As always I'd been too embarrassed to explain that it wasn't because I didn't want him with me; I'd simply wanted to spare him the vision of my soft surplusage. He hadn't spoken to me again before leaving for the airport. Not even to say good-bye.

"Smart move, Bloberella," I said. A hot, slow-moving tear slid down my nose and splashed onto my upper lip. I swiped it away with the back of my hand.

It wasn't only Jonathan's sudden bout of incommunicado that was bothering me. My reflection in the mirror forced me to admit that I was a failure on several fronts. Two years earlier, I'd made the move south to Durham from my original hometown of Boston with two goals in mind—to lose weight and to get hired as a TV reporter. I'd won the job, but now it seemed like I might be losing my edge. And I was heavier than ever.

Then go find an easier job, stupid. Become a fat, happy bread baker. Break up with Jonathan before he dumps you. Run away again.

My cell alarm beeped from deep inside my purse, interrupting my reverie of gloom and doom; it was 11:40. I'd have to scramble to make it on time for my lunch with Jana. No more time to gnaw at my paw with self-destructive thoughts.

I squeezed myself back into my waist cincher, then got dressed and tracked down Evelyn to say good-bye.

Minutes later I was threading my way through the mall parking lot toward my car. Tiny, dark crows of worry had started to gather at the edges of my thoughts about my relationship with Jonathan. Surely he'd banish all those shadows as soon as we had a chance to actually speak over the phone. Evelyn was probably right—I just had to have a little faith. And patience.

Unfortunately, patience has never been my strong suit. It's a character flaw that gets me into trouble all the time.

Chapter 3

Deep-six the Face Creams

Take all those mondo-expensive face creams you have in your cabinet, and toss them in the trash. I mean all of them (yeah, even that hundred-dollar thimble of sea cream). The beauty product marketeers will never cop to this, but none of those lotions and potions are worth a bucket of spit.

Clinically, the best skin cream for you in terms of protection and overall effectiveness is a zinc-based sunscreen.

—From *The Little Book of Beauty Secrets* by Mimi Morgan

An hour later I was huddled deep in the recesses of a corner booth at Becca's Bistro, still waiting for Jana to show. She'd called to say she was running late because her appointment with the plastic surgeon had run into overtime.

I was hiding my face behind an oversized leather menu, trying to avoid landing on the radar of reporter Lainey Lanston. I'd spotted my newsroom rival on my way into the main dining room. Her perfectly tailored back was turned to me, and she was engaged in a schmoozefest with a city councilman named Floyd McElroy.

Floyd was beloved by local reporters for his habit of leaking city hall gossip like a cracked gin bottle the moment he started his daily drinking ritual. And from the glow of the red moons waxing in his cheeks, I could tell that Floyd was already two fizzy gimlets to the wind.

The sight of them dining together filled me with dread. I wondered what kind of information Lainey was pumping from the councilman. I'd been planning to track down Floyd myself this morning, to discuss a lead I'd developed about the head of the city's animal control department who'd gotten caught up in a sex scandal. I'd held off calling him in order to shop for the goddamn bikini story and make my lunch with Jana.

Maybe Lainey had already gotten wind of the animal house allegations. Recently it felt as if she was shadowing my news sources—she'd even snatched a couple of major stories out from under me. If I was losing my edge, I might soon find myself replaced by Beatty's newest newsroom pet. What exactly would I *do* if I got canned? There wasn't another TV station in town—I'd have to move. What would that mean for my relationship with Jonathan? We'd never had a conversation about where we were going as a couple. Maybe that had been a mistake.

Jana appeared at the entrance to the dining room. "Hi, Kate!" she called out in a voice loud enough to soar above the din of the dining room.

She made a clacking trek across the stone floor in a pair of white slides and matching Bermudas. Behind her coppery bangs, her hair was sleeked back into in a low, short ponytail.

I peeked over the top of the menu to give her a smile and half wave, then sank back down to stay out of Lainey's line of sight—I could just imagine her smug expression if she spotted me having a civilian lunch with a friend while she was working a news source.

"Phew—that was totally depressing," Jana said, sliding into the upholstered booth opposite me. "I just had my 'before' pictures taken at Dr. Medina's office for my body lift. Thank God no one else ever sees those shots."

I stared at my slender friend in disbelief. "Why are you even thinking about having more plastic surgery, Jana? Those Bermudas are what, a size one? Your calves are like pencils. You look absolutely perfect."

Her mouth corkscrewed down on one side. "These shorts don't show it, but I have tons of loose skin on my upper thighs," she said. "I lost over a hundred pounds on the Fruit Diet, remember? Everything's hanging now, especially my breasts. Just ask Gavin—I'm sure he'll be *delighted* to tell you how disgusting I look naked."

"I'm sure Gavin doesn't think you're—"

Jana's face froze as a busboy brought us two glasses of ice water. When he withdrew, she shook her head firmly. "Our marriage is over, Kate," she said. "When he's not at the track, Gavin spends all his time on the computer. I found his password—I have to admit I was looking for it— and discovered a bunch of e-mails he sent to a girlfriend. Her name is Candy. *Candy*, can you believe that? How revolting. And here's the worst—he sent her naked videos of himself."

"Oh God."

"I gather she's not the first one, either. He told her how totally repulsed he is by the sight of me. He said my body looks like a Michelin tire woman that got the air let out." Squeezing her eyes shut, she turned her face toward the wall.

"Oh, Jana." Laying aside the menu, I reached across the table for her hand. "I'm so sorry."

Jana stared down at my hand on hers. "I really thought Gavin loved me," she whispered. "People were too polite to say it to my face, but I know everyone thought he was after my money. The only one brave enough to say it out loud was Shaina. She said she'd seen him with someone else while we were dating. That's why she wouldn't come to the wedding. I thought she was just jealous and trying to break us up."

Jana buried her head in her hands, then looked up at me. "How could I have been such an idiot? I was completely in thrall to him. Oh my God, Kate, the sex we had at the beginning was *incredible*. Actually it's *still* pretty good. It was never like that before with anyone else. How can a man fake that?"

"Don't put the blame on yourself. Love can make us blind." *Ugh. Why do love-gone-wrong conversations always come off sounding like song titles?* I wondered.

After a short silence, Jana said slowly, "You know what really bothers me? Gavin's online ID. I found him listed on a couple of those dating sites—he calls himself Shug, for 'sugar.' That was my pet name for him when we first met."

"What a bastard," I replied. "Of course, I'll retract that statement immediately if the two of you get back together."

She gave me a wan smile. "No chance in hell of that happening," she said. "Right now, I just want to strangle him."

Before I could respond, a tall waitress dressed all in black arrived at the table to take our order. I ordered a grilled chicken salad, Jana the spinach quiche.

When we were alone again, Jana said, "One more thing, Kate."

"Shoot."

"I'm pretty sure Gavin's been stealing money from me."

"*Stealing?*" Yikes. "How much?"

"About thirty thousand dollars is missing from one of our bank accounts. When I confronted him about it two days ago, he refused to discuss it. He knows I'm angry about it. Since then he's gone crazy with our credit cards. He's run up about fifty thousand dollars in cash advances. I just shut down all the credit cards a couple of hours ago."

Taking a deep breath, I said, "Jana, I think you need to consult a lawyer, not just me. Does your family have lawyers you can call?"

"No!" Jana shrank back from the table. "I can't tell anyone in Miami about my situation yet. If I tell my family's lawyers, it'll get right back to my brother, Belmont. I'm afraid he'll do something drastic."

"Like what?"

"I don't know. Belmont controls our family business, and he already thinks I'm immature about men. I don't even know what he could do, frankly. I just want to handle this divorce by myself, at least the initial stages. I've already acted enough like a fool."

I wasn't sure that "handling" a cheating, thieving spouse all by herself would make her seem any less foolish in her brother's eyes. But I would do whatever I could to help my friend.

After pausing for a moment to consider whether it would be wise to unleash a caveman on my genteel friend, I said, "I do know a guy who might be able to help. He's a former cop named Beau Fisher. Everyone just calls him Fish. He used to be on the Durham bunco squad."

"Bunco squad? What's that?"

"They bust confidence swindlers," I said, extracting my cell phone from my pocket to look up Fish's number.

"Confidence? That's perfect. Gavin swindled my trust in him big-time."

Tapping Fish's number into her own phone, Jana continued, "I'll call this guy Fish as soon as we finish lunch. I want to have the wheels in motion before I go back to Miami."

Sensing a shadow near my left elbow, I looked up. Standing next to me was the person I'd been trying desperately to avoid: Lainey Lanston.

"Well, he*llo* there, Kate." The reporter's caustic voice cut through the air and landed with a rattle against my eardrum. "Working hard, or hardly working?"

"Hi, Lainey," I said, not bothering not to roll my eyes. I looked over her shoulder for Floyd the councilman, but there was no sign of him. He'd probably drifted into the bar in search of an early-bird drinking buddy.

"The whole newsroom is buzzing about your new fat-scam series," Lainey said to me, then shifted her gaze to Jana. "We're just *dying* to see Kate in her swimsuit segment. Did she tell you about it?"

If I'd had any kind of segment in my hand right then, I'd have shoved it right up her mini-sized ass, which right then was encased in a ruffled, ruby red skirt topped by a jacket that was cut low enough to show plenty of cleavage. *Look at me; I'm so fine*, her outfit screamed.

"Well, stay tuned—it'll be worth waiting for," I said, stretching my lips wide enough to show plenty of teeth.

When I let a long moment pass without introducing her to Jana, Lainey's eyes narrowed.

"Well, I've got to go work on my county hospital piece," she said, checking in with the pager she had clipped to the outside of her patent leather tote bag. "Beatty just assigned it to me. Did you know? I guess you've been too busy. Enjoy your lunch, ladies." Without waiting for a response, she spun about on a spiked heel.

As Lainey marched away, Jana raised her eyebrows at me. "Was that a friend of yours?" she asked with a smile.

"Not even when she's pretending. Which she wasn't just then."

"Well, her boobage is really hideous. She should have gone to Dr. Medina for her breast implants."

"I *thought* Lainey's figure had changed since she switched from newspapers to TV," I said, suddenly wishing I'd studied her cleavage more closely. "But how could you tell she had implants?"

"You can always tell a cheap boob job by the mile-wide cleavage," Jana said. "Those saline sacs will be sliding down to her belly button by the end of the first year."

"Ah."

I tried to console myself with visions of Lainey being stuck with a boob job gone wrong, but her parting shot about taking over the county hospital story had left a smoking hole in my stomach. I'd just assumed the story was mine—a stupid assumption now that she was dogging my heels day and night. I'd already looked into charges that the hospital was dumping homeless people on skid row. It was going to be a huge story. *Her* huge story now.

Obviously Lainey had taken the lead on the fast track. She'd always been my major competitor for stories even when she'd worked in print. But things were worse now that she was digging her little stiletto heels into my home turf. Now she was more than just my competition. Now she was a threat to my job.

When the waitress came with our check, Jana mentioned that she'd lost her purse the night before.

"Can you believe this, Kate?" she said. "I feel just like one of those rich jerks who invites people out for lunch and then doesn't pay. I'm sorry."

"Don't be silly."

"Do you remember me having my purse at Trish's house? I thought I brought it there, but I didn't have it at the Hilton when I got back last night."

"Let's see," I said, trying to dig up a memory. "Did it have a woven metallic finish? Bronze colored?"

"Right! My Miu Miu bag—I *thought* I'd brought it in there with me last night," she said. "Okay, so I left it at Trish's house. No wonder; I was so distracted about seeing Shaina. Phew! I'll leave her another message, but I think she and Archer are leaving town. Maybe their son is still there. What's his name? D'you know?"

"Chaz, I think."

"That's right. Chaz must have answered when I called their house this morning. But when I mentioned my purse he just grunted and hung up."

"No surprise there," I said. "He's probably still out of it. I smelled pot on him last night. It was pretty strong."

"Uh-oh. I don't think Trish knows anything about that," Jana said. "But then, she's such a Gidget, she might thinks it's incense. According to her, the boy's highly gifted with computers, but a little low on the social IQ."

"Well, last night he would've scored high on a drug test," I said, reaching for the check.

Chapter 4

A Big Phooey on "Flat Belly" Diets

Oh, for Pete's sake! How many more fad diets will come along that try to open our wallets and extract cash in exchange for unproven claims that they target belly fat? Save your money. Here's what the average woman can do to trim her waist over time:

1. Cut 150 calories a day from your daily intake.
2. Walk at a brisk pace five days a week for twenty minutes, and build up to thirty minutes per day.
3. Start with a set of ten crunches on the first day, and add sets of ten until you build up to two hundred per day.

—From *The Little Book of Beauty Secrets* by Mimi Morgan

Something was definitely wrong.

When I returned to the studio that afternoon, I left not one, but *two* messages on Jonathan's cell phone. I had to handle some assignment-desk chores for Beatty while he recovered from an emergency root canal; meanwhile, I kept compulsively checking the messages on my landline at home. By five p.m., Jonathan still hadn't called me back. That would be ten p.m. in

London—plenty late enough for his mother to be asleep.

Before leaving the second message for him, I sought out the privacy of a sound booth. I perched on a stool, then listened with mounting tension to his greeting message. In the past, I'd always felt soothed by the sound of his voice, even in a recording. Not this time.

"Jonathan here," came his message. "Leave a word and I'll ring you back."

"But you're not ringing me back," I blurted after the beep. "It's me. Is your mom okay? Are *you*? Please call me as soon as you get this message. I love you."

My tongue tripped over the "I love you," three words that had always rolled off it so easily before. It was almost embarrassing how totally, completely consumed I was by Jonathan. Maybe that was why I'd always felt a little insecure about him. Maybe that was the real reason I'd never let him see me naked in the full light of day. If I didn't love my own body, why should he?

After leaving the second frantic message, I was afraid I'd come off like a clinging vine.

Fuck that thought—the man hasn't called you in a week. It's his fault. My Inner Girlfriend, who'd been feeling emboldened ever since that morning's shopping trip with the self-confident Evelyn, tried to prop me up.

But then Clinging Vine caterwauled, *There must be some reason he hasn't called you back. Maybe he's hurt. Maybe he's lying in a London ditch, dead.*

Jonathan hadn't given me his mother's phone number, and I didn't know a single friend of his in the UK whom I could call to check up on him. Not that I'd call them anyway—checking up on a guy with his friends is the quickest way to stamp your forehead with big neon letters that spelled *dumped*.

Workwise, the day had gone from bad to worse. As Beatty's fill-in, I had to review and approve every news story for the six o'clock show, including Lainey's. Just as I'd feared, she'd developed a piece—tipped off by Tipsy Floyd—about how the head of animal control had submitted his resignation over allegations of sexually harassing a city dogcatcher. The story was slugged, "The dog poop flies." It was scheduled to run as the lead that night.

Inside the production booth, I ran her story through a machine and reviewed her intro copy; the results were dreadful. Dreadful for me, that is.

Her story was great.

Chapter 5

Don't Try to be a Living Doll

Pity the woman who wants to look like a Barbie doll (yes, there are women out there who've actually paid big surgery bucks to transform themselves into living versions of the mammary-inflated toy).

If Barbie's measurements were translated into a real-life woman, she'd be more than seven feet tall, wear toddler shoes, and have an oversized head like an alien. Honestly, she'd be bizarre!

So the next time you want to look like a doll, or even a magazine cover, get ahold of yourself. (Pause to slap yourself across the face.)

Just concentrate on making yourself healthy and strong.

You got that, ladies?

—From *The Little Book of Beauty Secrets* by Mimi Morgan

I replayed Lainey's story. In addition to having a well-written piece, she looked absolutely perfect on camera. While other reporters made do with pancake makeup, Lainey used an airbrush wand to spray foundation on her face, neck, and hands so that all her skin tones were perfectly matched on high-definition TV. She had staked out permanent squatter's rights to the studio's green room, where she'd spend an hour at a time, painstakingly contouring her features with little brushes and pots of bronzers. But the effort paid off. People had been whispering, "network material," ever since Lainey had stepped into the newsroom.

Also network material was the little safari suit Lainey had donned for her stand-up. She looked ready to beam her next live shot from the Serengeti.

I shot a dispirited glance down at my own standard reporting gear—today I had on my expandable-waist black slacks, paired as usual from a rotating cast of V-necked tops in jewel colors. Today I was wearing cobalt blue to match my eyes. When assigned to cover a formal event, I'd throw on my good silk-and-rayon jacket from Nordstrom, which was roomy enough to cover my hips. Usually.

My cell phone vibrated in my pocket. It was Fish, the private investigator.

"I owe you a round, Kate. Hell, I owe you a night on the fucking town." The ex-detective's street-roughened voice boomed over a background thrum of clinking and bar chatter. "Your friend Jana Miller just wrote me out a check for eight grand. Any more socialites where she comes from? I could buy that fishing boat *and* an island."

I laughed and said, "Take it easy on her, Fish, okay? Jana's nice."

"Sure she's nice. It's the nice ones who can whittle away a man's balls until he's got nothing left but a pair of olive pits."

"I'll have to take your word for it on that one, Fish."

I heard a rattle of ice cubes as we signed off. I pictured Fish at the counter of the sports bar that had become his second home. Fish had the beetling brow of a Cape buffalo, plus a tendency to gore challengers when he got riled—or tanked.

Back when he was on bunco, Fish's drinking habit had fueled one too many bouts of street rage. The final straw had come when he bashed in the head of a con man who'd stabbed a police dog during an arrest. Both dog and suspect made full recoveries, but Fish had been deemed a psychological risk and was forced into early retirement.

I thought the con guy had richly deserved his punishment. Which means it's probably a good thing I didn't follow my father's example and become a cop. With my hair-trigger Irish temper, I might have actually blown off someone's head by now.

When the six o'clock news show wrapped, I smiled off an invitation from a couple of my reporter friends to join the nightly migration to our favorite watering hole, a restaurant called Bugtussles. At this point I was craving the solace of solitude, not shop talk.

My spirits rose when I reached the parking structure and saw my new car, a BMW Z4. I'd bought the silver sports coupe used, but its sharklike curves gleamed like it had just rolled off a showroom floor. My James Bond car, Evelyn called it. It was a wildly impractical machine to own, but fun as hell to drive.

When I pulled up in front of my house, I could just make out the edges of a furry, familiar profile. Elfie, my rag-doll cat, was posted at her usual spot in the bay window of the little foursquare house I'd rented a few months earlier in the Trinity Heights section of town.

Once inside, I clicked on the kitchen light. As if to reward my self-restraint for not checking my messages during the drive home, the red light on the answering machine on the faux-granite counter was blinking.

"Hi," a familiar voice began. It was Jonathan.

No "Hallo, luv," his usual salutation for me.

My boyfriend's voice sounded two degrees cooler than usual as he continued, "There's been

a bit of a cock-up with my schedule and I had to
change my plans—right now I'm not sure when
I'm coming back. Might be another week or two.
Keep you posted, all right?" he said. "Cheerio."

   Click.

Chapter 6

Cheerio?

I glared at the answering machine as if it could transmit my baleful energy through the undersea cables all the way to London, and deliver a thwack on my boyfriend's forehead. Where was his usual "I love you" or even "Miss you, luv"? There wasn't the slightest hint of affection in the message he'd left for me. What was up?

"What cock-up with your schedule?" I demanded of the machine. "What are you talking about?"

Obviously, Jonathan's mother wasn't dying. Obviously, he wasn't lying in a ditch someplace in a London slum. *Obviously*, he simply couldn't be bothered to call before now to let me know what the hell was going on with him.

A throbbing pulse began at my temples, then spread like a wildfire crackling across my scalp; I snatched up my cordless phone to call Jonathan back.

"Down, girl," I cautioned my temper before replacing the phone carefully in its base. What was the point of getting angry?

My mind leapfrogged to the worst-case conclusion about Jonathan's message: The answer must be that he was cooling off on me. I'd heard the tone of voice he'd used in his message once before in the past, from an old boyfriend who'd then proceeded to inform me that he was dumping me for the new TelePrompTer girl. But at least *that* guy had had the guts to deliver his message in person.

"What gives? First you avoid talking to me; then you leave me a cold-ass message like that?" I wailed at the answering machine, which sat in stony silence. "How cheesy. How *cowardly*. If that's all you have to say, then as far as I'm concerned you can—you can just . . ."

He could rot in hell.

In a fit of pique, I deleted Jonathan's number from my contact list. Okay, maybe that was an overreaction (and I had his number memorized anyway), but his frosty tone had hit me like a gut kick. He'd spoken like we barely knew each other. What the hell was going on?

Advancing farther into the kitchen, I threw open the refrigerator door. Foodwise, the view was barren except for some snap beans and heirloom tomatoes I'd picked up the day before at the farmers' market. And I was in no mood at that moment for anything healthy. I wanted something with a major sugar kick, and I wanted it *now*.

According to the wall clock, it was only ten p.m., which meant I still had time to make a run to Thirty-one Flavors for an emergency pint of Pralines 'n' Cream. Then my eye fell on a bottle of sauvignon blanc that was chilling on the shelf. I'd been planning to share it with Jonathan the next day to celebrate his homecoming from the UK.

There's nothing more sorry-ass than sitting at home alone, drinking over a guy who doesn't call, I told myself.

Defiantly I grabbed the bottle, then rummaged around in a drawer for a corkscrew. After a brief struggle to get the bottle open, I poured a generous amount of wine into a green-stemmed goblet.

"To relationships," I said, raising the glass in Elfie's direction. "Be grateful you're spayed so you don't have to play stupid mating games with tomcats. They'll let you down every time."

Elfie blinked her topaz blue eyes at me. Her expression was attentive but not overly empathetic. At times like this, it would be nice if Elfie were a dog, I decided. Dogs always seemed to understand when you're upset.

I decided to turn in. I made my way into the bathroom, grabbed my koala-bear sleep shirt from the hook on the back of the door, and changed into it. Then I brushed my teeth with vicious up-and-down strokes. After propping myself up in bed with a magazine, I sipped the glass of wine. It tasted sour after brushing my teeth.

I clicked on a cable news channel. I couldn't hear a sound over the thundering internal roar of my continuing mental rant at Jonathan. When I started to punctuate my thoughts with hand gestures, I cut myself off.

How pathetic, I thought. *Before long I'll be like Miss Lonelyhearts in* Rear Window, *getting piss-ass drunk and holding imaginary conversations with gentlemen callers.*

With a firm sense of resolve, I set the wine-glass down on the bedside table. There would be no getting drunk tonight for me. Not because I was afraid of becoming an alcoholic.

It's simply that when it came to getting an evil buzz on, no wine could ever give me a flavor-gasm like a pint of Pralines 'n' Cream.

Chapter 7

Why You Need to Shun the Sun

Worshipping the sun is so last millennium. The awful truth is, the sun pulverizes and ages your skin every time you step outside. You must always put on sunscreen before you venture outside, and the sunscreen must be the type that blocks both ultraviolet A (UVA) and B (UVB) rays. According to skin scientists, UVB causes sunburn and skin cancer, while UVA causes aging and some skin cancers.

Even if you wear sunscreen, you should still take other measures to protect your skin. Most sunscreens break down in the sun (which they don't tell you in the advertising). So you need to protect your skin with clothing as well as lotions—for example, take a cue from the ladies of yesteryear and buy yourself a pair of chic driving gloves. And bring a cute parasol or wear a protective hat when you're in direct sunlight for hours on end. That way your skin won't look like a leather feed bag by the time you're forty.

—From *The Little Book of Beauty Secrets* by Mimi Morgan

When the cell phone on my nightstand buzzed me awake at three a.m. Thursday morning, I grabbed for it eagerly, expecting it to be Jonathan. I wasn't awake enough yet to remember that I was mad at him. But instead of a London exchange, the LED displayed the number of the Channel Twelve news desk.

I stifled a groan. A call from work in the wee hours meant only one thing: a summons to roll out to cover a crisis someplace. Usually it would turn out to be nothing more exciting than a smoky fire. And every smoky fire looked identical. Seriously; you could use the exact same video to show every predawn smoker in the world and no one would be the wiser.

I answered the cell with my work greeting: "Gallagher."

"Hi, Kate—sorry, I know you're not on call tonight, but I've got something crazy going on."

It was the overnight news producer, Roe. Something "crazy" was *always* going on whenever Roe called. She monitored the police scanner like a jumpy little chicken hawk, pouncing on every squawk that came over the radio. Roe was an expert at working herself and everyone around her into balls of stress. She'd make an excellent news director someday.

"No problem, Roe. What've you got?" I was already turning over to click on the bedside lamp. The sudden burst of activity disturbed Elfie, who'd been curled up in a warm, sleeping lump at my feet. She lifted her head and gave me an offended glare.

"There's been a carjacking—the second one this week. This time it was on the good side of town, near the Hilton," Roe said in her usual rat-a-tat delivery style. "The victim is still at the scene. Cops are already there; ambulance is on the way."

"Where should I meet the crew?" I asked her.

"You don't have to; I've already sent another reporter to cover it. Here's why I'm calling you. . . ." Roe downshifted long enough to take a breath. "The victim just called here on the studio line. She was asking for you by name. It was a girl; she sounded really young. Her name's Shaina Miller? She claims to know you but didn't have your number."

"Shaina Miller?" For a moment, the name drew a blank in my sleep-fogged brain. Then it clicked. "You mean Jana Miller's daughter? I've never met Shaina, but I know who she is. Where's her mother? Where's Jana?"

"I didn't hear anything about a Jana. This girl, Shaina, was hysterical, and then we got cut off. I think the cops took the phone," Roe said. "This whole thing's a little off script for me. Are you going down there?"

"On my way." With my free hand, I stripped off my sleep shirt, then glanced around the bedroom for something to throw on. My eyes fell on a pair of ancient navy sweats that were draped over my stationary bicycle as a kind of permanent exercise bunting. They were seriously shlumpadinka, as Oprah would say, but I didn't have time to worry about it.

"Who's covering the carjacking story?" I asked Roe.

"Your favorite show horse."

"Oh, no. You mean Lainey?"

"Yeah, she's on call. And here's some more good news—it's raining like hell outside."

This time, I didn't bother to stifle my groan.

Chapter 8

Deep-Penetrating-Light Skin Therapy—
You be the Judge

One home-based skin-care machine on the market is a deep-penetrating-light machine. They're made by various manufacturers and are based on LED (light-emitting diode) technology. There's some science behind it, I gather, but I'm not sure it's worth three hundred to four hundred dollars, which is what some machines cost. I've been using it, but so far, I ain't groovin' on it.

—From *The Little Book of Beauty Secrets* by Mimi Morgan

The predawn scene that morning looked like many I'd covered in the past: police units stopped at crazy angles at the four points of an intersection, strobe lights throbbing through the mizzle; a luxury sedan—a Mercedes SL—that had its nose wrapped around a light pole; and under a dripping rain hood, peering through the cracked-open window of my Z4, a traffic cop who looked like he'd rather be walking the day beat.

"Lady, why didn't you pay attention to my signal?" Spittle blended with the rain runoff from the patrolman's hood. "It meant 'turn this damned car around and head the *other* way!'"

Lowering the window some more, I said, "I'm a friend of Shaina Miller. She asked for me. I'm Kate Gallagher, and I'm also a reporter for Channel Twelve. But I'm here as a personal friend for her, not professionally."

The cop blinked. Then grunted. "Stand by right here."

As my message got passed up a daisy chain of uniforms, I looked around for Jana or any young girl who might be her daughter, Shaina. But other than the emergency workers, there was no one in sight.

The message finally reached a cluster of emergency workers who stood huddled at the far side of the intersection. They were standing in a semicircle around a blue tarp that three patrolmen had spread out and were holding aloft with their hands several feet above the pavement, as if trying to protect the ground from the rain. A man in a dark rain poncho was half kneeling and shining a torchlight down at something on the asphalt. I couldn't see what he was looking at.

Another man in rain gear leaned away from the others and gave me a *come on over* wave. It was Detective Luke Petronella, a colleague of Jonathan's.

In *Homicide*.

Ignoring the traffic cop, I abandoned the car. Below my reporter's trench coat, my feet hit a puddle and instantly got drenched. The bottoms of my sweatpants sagged around my ankles as I jogged toward Luke.

The detective hurried forward to intercept me before I could reach the nucleus of the activity.

"*Luke?* Why are you here? What's going on?" I could feel the pressure of the next horrible question in my eyes.

That's when I caught my first glimpse of a still white form on the pavement, underneath the tent of blue plastic that the patrol cops were holding up. It was a woman's tiny form. I couldn't see her head, which was covered in a sheet. Her arms and legs were crumpled and spread akimbo across the pavement, bent at weird angles like a doll that had been flung from a speeding car. A pair of tanned legs protruded from below the covering. She was wearing familiar-looking white slides—one of them hanging askew off a twisted ankle—and matching Bermuda shorts. They looked like my friend Jana's shoes and shorts.

Confusion set in. I took a lurching step back. At the same time my mind scrambled for a way to reject what I was seeing.

"*No*, Luke." My hand flew up to cover my mouth. "That can't be Jana Miller. *Please* tell me that's not my friend."

Through the slit in his rain gear, Luke reached for my hand. "I'm sorry, Kate," he said. "A carjacker jumped her car when she was driving with her daughter. She managed to push her daughter out about a quarter mile from here, then apparently she fought with the guy until he plowed into that light pole over there. Then he must've gotten mad and pumped two bullets into the side of her head. She had no chance."

It's Jana. She's dead. Jana. Is. Dead.

Each awful word drove a furrow from one side of my brain to the other, until it crashed against the confines of my skull. For a moment I couldn't suck in any air—the pressure inside my chest cavity had escaped with a sudden release of breath. Bending over at the waist, I hung my head low and tried to recoup some precious oxygen. It felt as if a chunk of cement was blocking my throat, preventing airflow.

Luke placed his arm under my elbow. Like an iron T beam, for a moment his support was all that held me steady.

With my head still hanging near my knees, I craned my neck up to look at Jana again. The sight of her body lying on the pavement—soaked through despite the protective tarp that the patrolmen were holding above her—practically drove me into a frenzy.

"Why don't they put her into an ambulance now, Luke?" I pleaded with him, uncomfortably aware that my tone sounded nearly hysterical. "She's getting all soaked and cold down there on the ground. She shouldn't be put through this."

"Kate, there's nothing we can do for her anymore," Luke said. "My job now is to find who did this and put him in jail. Please let me call in a grief counselor for you." His normally brash, sarcastic voice was unusually gentle. I knew I was seeing his homicide-cop bedside manner.

"I know, Luke."

Hold on, Kate; the words flooded through my ear canal. It sounded like Jana's voice, as if she'd just stood up and shouted at me. *Hold* on, *dammit. My daughter needs you right now.*

It took a huge effort to straighten up. "Where's Jana's daughter, Shaina? My studio told me she called from here." My voice sounded strange and flat in my ears. But at least I'd stopped groping for air.

"She's okay—she has some bumps and bruises from being pushed out of the car. The EMTs gave her something to get her calmed down, and now she's on her way to Mercy."

As I stood staring wordlessly at Jana's body, Luke gave me an appraising look. "Shaina was not in any shape to identify her mother's body," he said. "I know it's a bad time, but I was wondering . . ."

"I can identify her," I said, again in that flatline voice.

"It's just a formality because we found her rental-car contract in the car. Are you sure you can you handle this, Kate?"

"I said I can *do* it, Luke."

The detective led me over to the blue tarp, where Jana's body lay. A woman wearing plastic gloves and a blue CSI jumpsuit nodded to me. I vaguely recognized her from covering other crime scenes. She knelt down next to Jana's body and pulled the sheet gently back from her head.

Jana's face was resting on its right side, facing toward me. Her eyes were open and sightless, her coppery short hair matted with dark blood that looked as thick as kindergarten paste. I'd once heard from an investigator that head blood is thicker than regular blood.

"That's her—that's Jana," I said.

The CSI woman lowered the sheet over Jana's face. "Your friend must have been a brave lady," she said, leaning back on her heels. "I heard she got her daughter out of the car before she got shot."

"I heard that, too. Thanks."

Go to Mercy now . . . you need to be with Shaina. Again, I had the eerie sensation of hearing Jana's voice in my ear. I turned toward my car.

The area surrounding the blue tarp suddenly lit up with a spotlight. I turned and saw a Channel Twelve broadcast van pulling up next to my car. They'd turned on the side floodlights, preparing to shoot the scene.

Luke swore under his breath. "Are you on the job right now, Kate? Because if you are—"

"No, I'm not," I replied. "I'm heading over to Mercy right now to find Shaina. The studio assigned the story to someone else."

"Who?"

As if in answer, the side door of the van slid back with a bang, and a videographer jumped out with his camera already rolling. Behind him, Lainey crouched in the van's doorway surveying the crime scene. I saw her neck arch back in surprise as she recognized me.

I looked at Luke. "You'll have to deal with Lainey, I'm afraid."

Luke shot a sour glance at Lainey. "No, I won't," he said. "That reporter really burned one of our guys on a story she did the other day. I'm not going to give her anything."

"Dandy by me, Luke. Handle her however you want."

Keeping my head down, I headed toward my car, hoping against hope that I'd make it to the Z4 before Lainey caught up with me. I slid into the seat and started to slam the door.

"*Kate!*" Lainey's hand caught hold of the top of the door's window. She held it in place with an iron grip while deftly inserting a hip between the door and me. "What's going on? That Mercedes over there was the car that was jacked, right? Why are you here?"

"I'm here on a personal matter, Lainey. The detective in charge is right over there. Luke Petronella. You can get all the details from him."

"Give me a break, Kate. This is the second carjacking this week. The fourth this month. Who was killed? I know you know what's going on. Help me out here with a little professional courtesy. Okay?"

"They're not releasing the victim's identity yet, Lainey. You'll have to wait. You know the drill."

"Forget the drill, Kate. This is a huge story, and you know it. So one person died? Was it someone you know, or are you working some angle of your own on this story?"

When I didn't reply, her mouth twisted into a snarl. "I know you're all tight-ass with the cops because of your boyfriend," she said. "But don't think you can hog every one of their stories that comes down the pike."

I wondered whether she'd chosen the verb "hog" on purpose. Probably.

"Jesus Christ. I'm not trying to steal your story, Lainey. I said I'm here because it's *personal*," I snapped. "You'll have to talk to the cops yourself. In fact," I said, my words picking up volume and heat, "why don't you go wiggle your butt right over there to the homicide detective and bat your eyes at him? I'm sure you'll get everything you want. Isn't that how you score most of your stories?"

Lainey flinched back. Her eyes narrowed, and then she took a step back from the car.

I closed the door with as much force as I could manage, then threw the Z4 into reverse. The tires screeched on the wet asphalt as I backed away.

Craning my neck to look over my shoulder, I steered the car in a reverse three-point turn. As I headed down the street and away from the scene, through the rearview mirror I could see Lainey still standing in the road, staring after me.

So okay; the ass-wiggling thing was a cheap shot I'd thrown in at the end. It wasn't even accurate, really. Lainey worked hard for her stories. But I still didn't like her. So sue me.

I knew I'd just turned a competitor into an enemy. But at the moment I had much more important things on my mind.

Right now I had to get to Shaina, Jana's daughter.

Chapter 9

Don't Become a Needle Junkie

Botox injections and fillers such as collagen can work wonders on crow's feet and marionette lines, but it's possible to overdo it. Lots of people don't know this, but having too many cosmetic injections can leave you with needle scars on your face, just like the tracks on a heroin addict's arms.

If you can't live without regular infusions of plumpers and fillers, consider getting fat injections by a board-certified plastic surgeon. Here's how it works: The surgeon draws a bit of fat from your stomach, then injects the fat into the crevices and wrinkles around your mouth and lips. Unlike collagen, your own fat acts as a long-lasting filler. And isn't that what we're all looking for?

—From *The Little Book of Beauty Secrets* by Mimi Morgan

I rode the elevator to the fourth floor of Mercy Hospital, then threaded my way through a confusing labyrinth of corridors following the scribbled directions I'd gotten from an emergency room receptionist. It was just past six a.m.; the hallways were slowly beginning to come alive with movement as nurses and technicians pushing blood pressure carts began their morning rounds.

Rounding a final corner, I spotted room 4D. Next to the half-open door was a small whiteboard with a name handwritten on it: Shaina Miller.

Tentatively, I pushed the door open the rest of the way.

Shaina lay curled up in a fetal position in the middle of the hospital bed. Like her mother, Shaina was tiny, with close-cropped, platinum white hair that was combed away from her face. Her eyes above her high, wide-set cheekbones were closed. The left side of her face looked raw and hugely swollen.

I stood at the foot of her bed, trying to decide what to do next. Then I heard a movement behind me.

"Are you a member of Shaina Miller's family?" A nurse asked, lightly tapping my arm. Her voice had a lilting Jamaican cadence to it. "We've been trying to locate them."

"I'm a friend of her mother's," I replied in a whisper. "My name's Kate Gallagher."

"You're Kate?" Shaina had bolted upright to a sitting position on the bed. Her eyes, wide-open now, were trained on my face. "The cops told me

Mom's dead. She's not dead, is she? She can't be. I didn't believe them."

Behind me, the nurse murmured something about going to find a doctor. Then she left the room.

I sat on the bed next to Shaina and took her hand. It felt icy cold.

"Shaina, your mom . . . ," I began haltingly, groping hard for the right words. In this case, though, there could only be wrong ones.

Shaina made a choking noise and fell back against the pillow. Turning her head toward the wall, she said in a dull, flat voice, "For a second, I told myself this was all a bad dream. A nightmare."

"I'm so sorry," I said. "The emergency responders couldn't do anything for your mom, Shaina."

Still staring at the wall, Shaina said, "It happened so fast. Mom and I had stopped at a stop sign."

"You don't have to talk about it right now."

She continued as if I hadn't said anything. "That's when that guy—that *fucker*—broke in the window on Mom's side of the car. She screamed at me to get out; then she pushed me out the door."

Shaina looked at me, tears welling in her green

eyes. "My mom—she pushed me out the door. My mom saved me, Kate," she whispered.

"Your mother was very brave."

"I fell on the side of the road. I think the hijacker got the wheel, and Mom wound up on the passenger side, where I'd been. That's when I lost sight of them. A few seconds later I heard two shots. Then a car squealing, like it was driving away fast."

Her entire body seemed to quake with a sob as she added, "Why did it have to be my mother? She's all I have in the world."

A pain ricocheted off my ribs and hit something deep and soft inside my chest. "Shaina, I know this is a horrible time for you," I said to her. "I'm going to stay with you until your family gets here."

"My *family*?" Shaina made a bitter-sounding noise. "There's no one in my family except for Mom."

"What about your uncle?"

"Uncle Belmont and my aunt?" Shaina gave me a beseeching look. "They're not the same; you know what I mean? We're not that close. Nothing like my mom."

She made a disgusted noise in the back of her throat. "Then of course there's my stupid stepfather—Gavin the gigolo. Like *he's* gonna care about me at all. Mom told me last night they were getting divorced. She was dumping him. It was about time."

"Shaina, you can't help feeling unbelievably sad right now," I said, trying to ignore what she was saying about her stepfather. "It hurts so much. Believe me I know—I lost my mom, too, when I was young. To violence like your mom."

"You did? But then, you're still young, aren't you?" Shaina gave me a trembly attempt at a smile. "I don't think you're all that much older than me. You just act kind of older."

"I was thirteen."

"Oh my God. That *was* young."

"Any age is tough to lose your mother."

I knew this wasn't the right time to ask her questions, but an irresistible urge overcame me. "Why were you and your mom out driving so early this morning?"

"Mom was taking me to catch an early flight to Los Angeles," Shaina said. "She was going to follow me out there in a couple of days. We were going to take a cruise together."

Already regretting the impulse to probe, I quickly said, "I spoke to one of the detectives, and they're doing everything they can to track down the person who did this. They'll find him, and he'll be punished."

Shaina studied me. She was no longer crying,

and the surface of her eyes had turned as hard and flat as malachite.

"The police don't need to look for him." Her voice was cold and sounded much older than her twenty-one years. "I already know who killed my mother."

Chapter 10

Beware the Botched Boob Job

Breast enhancement is one of the most popular cosmetic procedures around. I mean, c'mon—who doesn't dream of being a centerfold fantasy? But you need to be careful before you mess with your breasts. A lot can go wrong with breast implants, and often does.

There are a couple of telltale signs of poorly done breast implants:

- *Bad placement—The breasts look too far apart, or they hang too low or too high.*
- *Ripple effect—The skin turns wrinkly around the nipples and underarms.*
- *Hardening—The breasts feel hard due to the formation of scar tissue around the implant.*

To avoid undesirable results, make sure you see a board-certified plastic surgeon before undergoing any surgery, and discuss in detail how your implants will appear.

—From *The Little Book of Beauty Secrets* by Mimi Morgan

Shaina's words sent a cold drip of sweat running down my spine. "You're saying you *know* the man who hijacked your car?" I said. "You mean the one who shot your mother?"

"No, but I know who was *behind* the whole thing. It was my stepfather, Gavin. I'm positive of it. He paid that guy to kill her. Maybe he even wanted both of us dead. I wouldn't put anything past him."

Her accusation shocked me. "Shaina, I know your mother and Gavin had problems, but why do you think he had anything to do with—"

"It was Gavin; I'm telling you. He did it to get her money before she could divorce him. It was Gavin! *Gavin!*" With each repetition of her stepfather's name, Shaina's volume and pitch rose until she was practically screaming.

At that moment, the nurse reappeared at the doorway. In tow behind her was a tall and kindly looking woman wearing a white doctor's coat. The doctor moved swiftly to Shaina's bedside.

"Shaina? I'm Dr. Sanders," she announced. "The nurse is going to give you something to help you feel a little bit more relaxed, and then you're going to sleep for a while."

As the nurse prepared a syringe, Shaina writhed on the bed, moaning and calling for her mother.

The doctor caught my eye and motioned for me to step outside the room. She followed me into the hallway, then said, "I appreciate your being here, but it's best for Shaina to simply sleep right now. Her stepfather is on his way here, along with someone else in her family."

"Do you think she should see her stepfather after what she just said about him? She seems to think he's behind her mother's murder. I'm wondering if we should—"

Dr. Sanders dismissed my question with a wave of her hand. "Paranoid thinking is common during the first stages of shock and grief," she said. "Victims want to blame someone, and they often focus on someone with whom there's been some family tension. It doesn't mean anything. By tomorrow, she won't even remember saying any of that."

As I hesitated, she added, "You should probably head home for a while—we've given her enough medication to make sure she'll sleep for at least eight hours. I suggest you come back around two o'clock this afternoon to see her."

When I looked in on Shaina again, her eyes were closed and she was pulling in deep, raggedy breaths, as if she were still sobbing in her sleep. Then the medication must have kicked all the way in, because her breathing rhythm gradually evened out.

The nurse who'd been monitoring Shaina's pulse looked down at her and made a clicking noise with her tongue against the roof of her mouth.

"This poor little lamb is going to have a very hard time," she said to me. "Imagine a young girl losing her mother like that. It's a horrible thing. It should never happen that way."

"I know."

"There've been so many carjackings recently," the nurse said. "It's getting to where we're all afraid to drive around at night."

Reluctantly, I decided that the doctor was right—it was time for me to go. There was nothing I could do for Shaina right then. I decided to return in the afternoon to see how she was doing.

I headed back to a space of tree-lined curb stretching beyond the emergency room area, where I'd left my car parked illegally. A few threads of citrine light were beginning to probe the edges of the horizon, but it was still dark in this area.

I was so lost in thought that I didn't pay any attention to a pillar-shaped shadow behind my car. Then the pillar moved. It stepped forward and grabbed my arm.

I let out a startled scream. Using the hand that was wrapped around my keys, I lashed out with an uppercut.

My jab was stopped in midair by something that felt like a baseball mitt; then my fist was gently lowered back to my side.

"Cripes almighty, Kate; if you've been taking self-defense courses, get a refund."

The voice belonged to Fish, the private detective. He released my hand from his ham-hock grip.

"Dammit, Fish. Let a person know you're standing there next time," I said, struggling to bring my hammering pulse under control. "Didn't your mother teach you not to sneak up on people?"

"My mother was too busy flattening my ass with a frying pan to give me that little tip. And here's one for you—you should learn to be more aware of what's going on around you."

"Thanks, Pop. I needed that."

"How's Jana's daughter doing?"

"Her doctor gave her some heavy-duty meds, so she's sleeping right now. Physically she seems okay, I guess. Lots of bruising. She got pretty hysterical right before they put her under."

"Did you find out where the two of them were headed when their car got jumped?"

"To RDU Airport. Shaina told me her mother was driving her to catch a plane to L.A. Evidently they were going to meet there later and take a cruise together."

Fish slammed his fist into his palm. "Goddammit, just like I thought. It's my fault. *I'm* the one who told Jana to leave the country for a while," he said. "Those motherfuckers are going to regret this. Now they've gone and killed my client. *My* client. I'm going to make them sorry they were ever born."

"Why do you say 'they'? Shaina saw only one guy."

"These scumbags always work in packs. They're friggin' jackals."

He cocked back his boot, then landed a vicious kick on the rear tire of my car.

"Knock it off, Fish," I said, putting a restraining hand on his arm. "It's not your fault, and tearing up my car isn't going to bring Jana back."

Fish looked sheepish. "Sorry, Kate. Nice ride, by the way," he said. "You must be climbing up the social ladder."

"The only thing that's climbing up the social ladder right now are my car payments."

After a beat I added, "A moment ago you said 'packs.' Do you mean gangs?"

"No question about it," Fish replied. "I've heard there's one GPDU gang behind most of the car-jackings in Durham this month."

"GPDU? What's that?"

"Gratuitous public display of underwear. You know—the saggers and baggers."

"Yeah, I know. Those are the guys who like to dress like they're high on plumber's crack. Pants hanging all low."

"You got it."

I decided to tell Fish about what Shaina had said about her stepfather, Gavin—that he was behind her mother's murder.

"Shaina seemed convinced that he was behind the carjacking—she said that he wanted them both killed. The doctor said that was the hysteria talking. What do you think?"

Fish took a moment to consider. "On its face, that notion is pretty far-fetched. Most crimes are just what they seem to be, and this one walks and talks like a simple carjacking."

"You don't make that sound very convincing."

Fish ground some loose asphalt under the toe of his boot. "Let me think about this a bit more before I go shooting my mouth off. I don't want to say anything that'll turn out to be from left field."

"C'mon, Fish," I said, my tone urgent. "Talk to me. Jana was my friend. I need to know what's going on."

He sighed. "Okay, but this is only for your ears," he said. "In the few hours I was working the case, I was able to dig up a few real nasty tidbits about that husband of hers, 'Gavin.' For example, he changed his name to Gavin from Guido. And he didn't grow up in Europe— he was raised in Boston. What a low-life piece of work. That's why I advised Jana to take a vacation. I wanted her out of the way for a while."

"Why?"

"Jana told me that Gavin's first wife died in a car accident in Omaha. But she evidently didn't know that his previous wife's accident was considered suspicious."

"Suspicious how?"

"There was a bunch of stuff that didn't add up. I talked to a detective in Omaha. He told me they couldn't make a solid case, so no one was ever charged."

I felt a storm front move through my stomach. "Did the police suspect *Gavin* in that woman's murder?"

"Yup. Evidently they were really going after him, and so was the life insurance company. But they finally dropped it for lack of evidence. The insurance company eventually paid him off."

"How much did he get?"

"Four hundred thousand dollars. The instant he blew through all that money he married Jana."

"But she told me over lunch yesterday that she has a prenuptial agreement. Wouldn't that—"

"A prenup only protects her assets while she's alive. She left him a very healthy life insurance policy. What a colossal mistake her high-priced attorney let her make. I told her to change the beneficiary before she left town. I hope to hell she did."

"How healthy?"

"Two million dollars."

That could be two million reasons for murder.

Chapter 11

Keep the Air Moist in Winter Months

It's important to moisturize your skin during the winter months. It keeps your skin looking soft, and studies suggest that moisture helps suppress the spread of flu virus in the winter. You can even try your grandmother's trick of heating an air-moisturizing kettle on the stove.

—From *The Little Book of Beauty Secrets* by Mimi Morgan

After leaving Mercy Hospital, I drove home through a thick southern mist, the kind that clings to the car and makes you try your windshield wipers in vain. But at least the monsoons had lifted. The morning rush-hour traffic reminded me that it was still early in the day, which seemed oddly surprising; eons seemed to have passed since I'd been jolted awake by Roe's telephone call.

Inside my kitchen I made a pot of coffee while mulling over what I'd learned about Jana's husband, Gavin. Could he have arranged her death as some kind of hit for hire? As a reporter I'd covered plenty of stories where murder had been committed for much less gain than a two-million-dollar insurance policy. Especially if he'd known that she was planning to leave him, Gavin had plenty of motive to arrange her death.

I yearned to talk to Jonathan. He'd know instinctively whether there was any real cause for suspicion about Jana's husband. Probably he'd tell me not to worry about it—that Luke was a great cop, and that the evidence would steer the investigation.

Before trying Jonathan, I put in a call to Evelyn and told her what had happened.

As soon as she recovered from the immediate shock about Jana's murder, Evelyn promised to call our friends in the Durham area to give them the tragic news.

Except for Trish. I needed to call her myself.

During our last conversation, Jana had mentioned that she'd left her purse behind at Trish's house on the night of the Newbodies meeting. I didn't know whether she'd had a chance to reclaim the bag before the carjacking. It was a beat in the story that sounded off, like an engine misfiring a cylinder.

Evelyn, who'd put down the phone to print out her contact list, returned to the line.

"Oh, Kate," she said. "Everyone in our group

is going to be so incredibly devastated when they hear about Jana. And frightened."

"By the carjacking, you mean?"

"By the fact that it's happened again to our support group. Jana is the second member of the Newbodies to be killed."

Chapter 12

"Someone *else* was killed?" I asked Evelyn. "Who? How come I never heard about it?"

"I didn't know her," Evelyn replied. "Her name was Anaïs Loring. She died last spring right before I joined the Newbodies. Anaïs was the group's founder. Everyone said she was very charismatic."

"Was it a carjacking?"

"No," she said. "Anaïs was killed in a home-invasion robbery. There was lots of stuff stolen from her home, including her jewelry and credit cards. Anaïs was found shot dead in her kitchen."

The story rang a distant bell. I must have heard about the Anaïs Loring murder at the time. I'd have to look it up when I got back to the studio. Talk about being behind the times.

While I was thinking, Evelyn continued. "The police never arrested anybody in Anaïs's murder," she said. "And now *Jana*'s dead. And last week another woman in our group got her identity stolen. So I'm thinking—"

"Wait a second. Slow down, Evelyn," I said as her implication sunk in. "You think the two murders—of Jana and Anaïs—are linked? A home invasion and a carjacking? And that the killings are connected somehow to the identity theft of another woman in the group?"

When Evelyn didn't respond, I added, "Identity theft usually happens when someone logs on to a bad Web site on the Internet. What makes you think it has anything to do with Jana? Or Anaïs?"

"I don't know exactly," Evelyn admitted. "But it feels like some evil karma is stalking the New-

bodies. I'm even wondering if we should disband the group."

When my conversation with Evelyn wrapped
up, I punched in Jonathan's number. I was already mentally rehearsing the message I wanted
to leave, the precise words that would let him
know how urgent it was that I speak to him right
away.

Jonathan surprised me by picking up on the
third ring.

"Hallo," he said.

"Hi, sweetie; it's me."

A slight pause. "Of course. How've you been?"
Jonathan's tone was stilted.

"Well, I just wanted to reach you in general," I
began, thinking how lame my words sounded.
"And especially today, because something has
happened."

"Oh." Another weird pause. "Kate, I'm sorry,
but is it okay if I call you right back? I'm—"

From his end of the line I heard a strange
noise. It sounded like the trilling sound a caged
bird makes. Then there was a muffled sound, as
if Jonathan was covering the receiver with his
hand. Or maybe someone was trying to grab it
from him.

"Is everything all right with you there?" I

asked, worried now. "Is it your mother? Is she okay?"

"Mum's fine. I've just been busy because some things came up. I'll call you when I—"

Another sound of a struggle that ended in a peal of female laughter. Then a different voice came on the line. It was a woman's voice.

"Katie, honey, Jonathan's busy right now." She sounded extremely young, and she spoke with an Asian-sounding accent.

Then she added with a giggle, "You've heard of me, right, Katie? My name is Gi. I'm Jonathan's wife."

My heart tumbled into my gut.

"But why don't you call me Gigi?" she continued. "That's what my Johnnie calls me."

I tried to think of something to come back with. But I was completely speechless. I couldn't even move my lips.

Meanwhile Gi—*Gigi*—continued speaking in a bright, oddly chipper tone: "Ooh, did Johnnie forget to tell you he's still married? His bad. I'll spank him now for you, okay? He likes that. We're fucking like love bunnies right now."

In the background, Jonathan yelled, "Cut it out, Gi. Damn you."

Then he came back on the line, his voice urgent. "Kate, let me explain. This is not what you—"

I couldn't bear to hear anything more. There would be. No. More. Words.

I slammed down the receiver.

Chapter 13

Straighten out Your Eye Circles

Nothing says "old and tired" like dark circles underneath your eyes. While some of us have a genetic predisposition toward eye circles, there are remedies and concealment tricks galore.

Here are a few of my tried-and-true techniques:

- *Get plenty of sleep. Too often, many of us get shortchanged on z's. Make sure you get seven or eight hours of sleep on a regular basis.*
- *Don't skip your exercise—poor circulation exacerbates circles.*
- *Drink lots of water—dehydration makes circles worse.*
- *Use a concealer with a pink tint to mask gray-tone circles.*
- *Stay moisturized—try rubbing a bit of almond oil under your eyes every night and every morning.*

—From *The Little Book of Beauty Secrets* by Mimi Morgan

I gaped down at my hand that was resting on the phone, trying to absorb what I'd just heard. Then my palm felt a vibration. It was the phone ringing—Jonathan trying to call me back.

Abruptly, I picked up the receiver and banged it down again to cut him off. Then I unplugged the cord from the wall. There would be no more talking. Not now.

In a daze, I dropped onto a stool by the kitchen counter. For a long while I simply perched there, staring silently into space. My brain was too stunned to think—all it could do was reel from the shockwaves.

Gi.

It was a name I knew well. Gi, Jonathan had told me when we'd first met, was his ex-wife. He'd never said much about her, only that she was a refugee from North Korea, and that their marriage had ended when he'd discovered that she was having an affair. Jonathan had never been willing to talk about her much, and I hadn't pried. But once when I was over at his apartment I'd found a picture of her. The photo had showed Gi wrapped in the arms of a beaming Jonathan. He'd been staring down at her with obvious adoration—and more than a little lust. (*Had he ever looked at* me *that way?* I'd wondered at the time.)

Gi had delicate features and huge dark eyes that were set in an alabaster complexion. She looked like an Asian Audrey Hepburn. Gorgeous as hell.

My first thought when I'd stumbled across the picture of them together was *How can the man who loved this incredible beauty be satisfied with someone who is overweight and out of shape? How can he want me after Gi?*

The answer was obvious to me now. He'd never wanted me at all. He'd never really left her, in fact. On the phone Gi had said that she was Jonathan's *wife*, not his ex-wife. Could that possibly be? Had Jonathan lied to me when he'd said they were divorced? Did I even *know* this man, really? Maybe he'd been covering up a long-distance marriage to Gi all this time. Plenty of guys did that, I knew. I just hadn't thought that Jonathan was that kind of guy.

I cast back on every conversation we'd had about Jonathan's marriage to Gi. There hadn't been many of them. In fact, it had been Jonathan's resolute silence on the subject of Gi that had always fueled my insecurities about our relationship. On some level I figured he'd never gotten over her. And, boy, had I gotten *that* one right. It was obvious now that he'd never left her at all. Jonathan and Gi were still married. *Married.*

So what precisely did that make me?

"You're an idiot, Kate; that's what you are. A

fool, *un estupido*," I muttered out loud. "You were just an easy port of call for Jonathan. A no-stress lay. Dammit dammit *dammit . . .*"

I'd made everything so easy for him. I'd been so-*o* Miss Independence with my TV news career, never pressing to know where our relationship was headed. I'd never asked, because I hadn't known where I was headed myself, careerwise. It had never occurred to me that I was just the right type of woman for a man who wasn't looking for a permanent relationship. That I was an easy target for a liar.

That's when the anger broke loose. No crying yet—that would undoubtedly come later.

"A *liar*, that's what you are," I yelled at the phone.

As Elfie jumped and skittered from the room, I added, "You're a moldy-faced, stinking liar, Jonathan. I *trusted* you!"

In the wake of that outburst, cold fingers of nausea moved into my stomach, probing its edges. They worked their way slowly up my throat muscles. Then a wrenching spasm turned my insides out. I stumbled in the direction of the bathroom.

I spent the next couple of minutes retching my guts out into the toilet. There wasn't much to come up—even though I'd been up since three a.m., I hadn't eaten anything since the night before.

When my stomach was empty, I dry heaved a couple of times. Then I rested my throbbing forehead against the lid. I was already totally exhausted, and the day had barely started.

Something soft and sinewy brushed against my cheek. I lifted my head from the toilet and saw Elfie peering into my face.

Raising her right front paw in the air, my cat mewed and gently touched my cheek.

"What's *wrong* with you?" she was obviously saying in cat-speak.

"Well, Elfie," I said, stroking her back. "It's nice to know that someone still loves me."

Now that she had my attention, Elfie sat back on her haunches and began grooming her long, drooping white whiskers. She always looked like a walrus when she did that.

Gazing down at my kitty, I felt engulfed by a wave of tenderness. It was an emotion that reminded me that once, I had dared to let myself dream about having children with Jonathan. I'd felt certain that he would be an amazing father.

Well, that dream was now officially dead. The anger and nausea receded and a new emotion—sadness—engulfed me. It was more than sadness, really.

That's when the tears began to flow. They built until, volumewise, the downpour of earlier that day was a mere sprinkling by comparison.

When Evelyn described the four cycles of love at the Newbodies meeting, she'd forgotten to mention a cycle.

She'd forgotten the cycle called grief.

Chapter 14

To Knock him Dead, Wear Red

The color red drives men wild, scientists have discovered. A study by psychologists at the University of Rochester revealed that the color red makes men feel more amorous toward women. And here's the best thing—the study suggests that men are totally unaware of the role that color plays in their attraction.

For centuries, rosy hues have been associated with the rituals of love and carnal desire, from Valentine's Day hearts to red-light districts. In the study, men were more attracted to pictures of women when they had a red border around them, or when they wore a red shirt, than they were to pictures of the same woman with borders or shirts of different colors.

Evidently there is a biological basis for the aphrodisiacal effect of red—in the wild, male primates are also attracted to females displaying red, which increases in females around the time of ovulation.

So, gals, take advantage of this little beauty secret. If you want your date to drool over you at dinner, break out your best red dress or sweater. While you're at it, add a pair of red shoes!

—From *The Little Book of Beauty Secrets* by Mimi Morgan

I arrived at the Channel Twelve studios just before ten a.m. Thursday morning, clutching a light latte that I'd picked up on the way. I trudged on autopilot from the parking structure to the newsroom, almost unaware of my surroundings. My emotions were too busy reeling from the blows of Jana's death and Jonathan's betrayal. The only thing I had left in my emotions bank was an overdraft.

The newsroom was suspended in its morning lull between the end of the morning report and the ramp-up to the midday news. Reporters were scattered about shooting the bull or hunched over newspapers. The one person who appeared to be actually working was the summer intern, whose job it was to monitor breaking news. She was sitting in a swivel chair making notes in front of a bank of screens that were tuned to cable TV stations.

I scanned the whiteboard. To my relief, I saw that I hadn't been assigned to work on anything yet that day. All I needed to do was make a few calls before getting back to the hospital to check on Shaina.

"Tell the desk not to put me on anything today. I'm here today, but not really," I announced to Rob, the studio director. He was dubbed Jumpy Rob for the way he constantly ejected from his seat in the control room while screaming camera directions into his headset.

Rob didn't even look up from the TelePromp-Ter scripts he was laying out on a large desk in the middle of the bullpen.

"Gallagher, here today but not really," he echoed. "Doing a little legwork on your bikini story, are you?"

"It's not a bikini story," I retorted. "I'm doing a five-part series about weight-loss scams."

"But the bikini's the money shot." He bent his head low to sniff at a page of script. "What's *this*?"

Picking up the script between two disdainful fingers, he demanded of the newsroom at large, "Someone calls this an intro?"

As Rob crumpled the offending intro into a ball and tossed it into a trash can, I trudged across the carpeted floor to my cubicle and threw my purse at the desk. My aim was off, and it thumped against the cubicle wall.

"*Hey!*" Crystal protested from the other side of the wall. "You made me spill my double espresso."

Crystal is a former public defender who traded in her attorney briefs for an on-air career as a legal reporter. The camera loves her quartz gray eyes and caramel complexion. She's the only one of us who dares to go on the air without foundation.

Poking her head over the cubie wall, Crystal said, "Bad day already?"

Then taking a look at my face, she added, "Uh-oh. We'll talk as soon as I finish this script."

I couldn't muster a reply as I checked my cell phone messages. One from Evelyn was marked urgent. She said there was going to be a gathering of the Newbodies later that day in the Duke Forest. The Newbodies were going to have a Memory Ceremony to honor Jana.

Frank poked his head into my cube. Frank's my favorite videographer. He's only five foot six, but he's got the muscled shoulders and bulldog stance of a heavyweight.

"I've been looking for you, Kate," he said. "What the heck happened between you and Lainey last night? The overnight crew said she was stomping around this morning, claiming you made her screw up her carjacking story. She says you told the police not to speak to her."

Stifling a grin, he added, "Beatty was all over her ass because we got scooped by news radio."

"A friend of mine was killed in that carjacking," I replied. "Lainey and her scoop can go piss in the goddamn wind as far as I'm concerned."

Frank's expression turned serious. "I'm really sorry to hear about your friend," he said. "I heard there were two victims. I heard that on the *radio*, mind you."

"Her daughter's alive but still in the hospital. In fact, I need to head back over there to be with her. I guess I'm not thinking straight—I can't even remember why I came in here right now."

My voice dissolved into something dangerously close to a sob. It's always been a point of pride with me never to cry in front of my colleagues. But Jana's murder and the abysmal phone call with Jonathan had spun my world on its axis. I felt spent and dangerously off-kilter. The floodgates of emotional hell had swung wide open, and the devil dogs were on the loose.

Crystal must have heard the SOS in my voice, because suddenly she also materialized in the opening to my cubicle. "Time for a confab in the ladies' room," she said, shooing Frank away. "Let's go."

We retreated to the ultimate sanctuary—the handicapped stall in the women's restroom.

"Tell me about what's going on, sweetie," she said. "Is it about your friend? I heard there was a carjacking overnight. I know that must be upsetting."

Crystal unwound a length of toilet tissue and handed it to me. In moments of stress, Crystal has a calm, maternal side that's oddly comforting. You feel like you could lean your head against her shoulder and cry your eyes out, and everything would be better.

"Yes, my friend Jana died. But there's a lot more going on," I said, finally yielding to the sob. "It's Jonathan. I know it's stupid to be upset about a guy when someone has died . . ."

"Nothing's stupid when it comes to love, honey."

"I caught Jonathan in bed with his wife this morning. According to her, they're still married."

"His what? His *wife*?" Crystal looked confused. "Wait—how did you catch them in bed together? I thought Jonathan was in the UK."

"He is. It was over the phone. He sounded completely weird when I called him, and then his ex-wife—or maybe they're still married. I don't know, she *called* herself his wife—grabbed the line. Gi's her name. She said they were f-f-fucking like l-l-love bunnies."

"And they're still *married*?"

"That's what she said."

"Well, don't believe every woman who grabs a phone away from a man. But if he really was in bed with her, he should rot in hell." Crystal wrapped me in a hug. "Oh, honey, I'm so sorry. Go ahead and let it out."

"I wish Jonathan was right here, right now, just so I could peck out his eyeballs bit by bit, like a bird. I'd peck them out." I formed a pair of pincers with my fingers to demonstrate what I'd do to Jonathan.

"It sounds like there's a pair of balls on the *other* end of him you should peck off first," Crystal said, her tone dry. "Anyway, eye pecking is something you should definitely do in the privacy of home. That's what I always do when I find out my man's a rat. And I've had more than a few."

"You have?" I said, blowing my nose loudly into the tissue. "It's so hard to believe that Jonathan's a rat. You know him, Crystal. He's always been so perfect, such a gentleman to me. How can he be a rat?"

"Well, man-rats don't all have whiskers and red, beady little eyes," Crystal said, wrinkling her nose like a mouse. "It's the sweet, gorgeous men like Jonathan that can really hurt you bad."

"This is more than hurt," I said, perching in a doubled-over sitting position on the edge of the toilet. "This feels like something's changed in my DNA . . . like my cell structure is going haywire. Pardon me a second . . ."

The wrenching stomach pain had come back, worse than before. Abruptly, I dropped to my knees on the cool tile floor and turned to face the toilet. Then I threw up again. This time all I could manage was weak-sounding, raspy little heaves.

"Sorry," I gasped and spat into the bowl. "This is so *un*believably humiliating."

"We've all totally been there, honey. Let me take you home," Crystal said. "You need to get some rest."

"Can't," I said, shaking my head. "My friend's daughter needs me at the hospital. Her family hasn't gotten here yet."

"Well, just remember you need to take care of yourself," Crystal said. "You're not in good shape yourself. That's a heavy load you're carrying around right now."

As she gave me soothing pats, she said, "Men. Sometimes I want to just ship 'em all off to Alaska. Put them out to pasture with the moose."

Before I escaped from the newsroom, I had to endure one more blow to my system. When I returned to my cubicle, I saw that someone had dropped something on my desk. A photo.

The five-by-seven-inch picture showed an enormously obese woman. She must have been at least four or five hundred pounds and was mostly naked, with giant, dimpled thighs and layers of flesh that stretched from her chin to her ankles. Though it was almost hidden among the overlapping layers of hanging fat, you could see that she was wearing a bikini. That image alone was grotesque enough. But that's not all there was.

Across the fat lady's distended stomach, in jagged strokes of a black Sharpie, someone had scrawled two words:

Kate Gallagher

Chapter 15

If you need a quick fix for puffy eyes, try cold packs and cucumbers. This old remedy really does work! Also, keep in mind that you need to get plenty of rest, plus lots of water. You also shouldn't drink too much alcohol—but hey, you already knew that, didn't you?

—From *The Little Book of Beauty Secrets* by Mimi Morgan

As I stared down at the grotesque image of the fat lady in the photograph, my scalp prickled with humiliation. Was that fat-lady picture—with my name on it—somebody's sick idea of a practical joke? Who could possibly want to hurt me like that? Who could be so vicious?

A vision of Lainey's angry face from the night before floated through my head.

Lainey. Of course. Frank had told me that she blamed me for keeping her from getting her precious carjacking story. Who else could it have been?

I thought back on Jumpy Rob's smirk as he

mentioned my story's "money shot"—aka me in a bikini. Was the entire newsroom secretly laughing at me? When the story aired, would the entire *city* make fun of me? The thought made me feel like throwing up again. At this rate, I wouldn't have to worry about dieting—the way I was barfing all over the place, I was well on my way to becoming bulimic.

Well, at least I didn't need to worry about Jonathan's reaction to my body in the story anymore. That dog in my heart had already died.

I tossed the disgusting photo into the trash. Then I put in a call to Luke Petronella to see what was going on in the investigation into Jana's murder. I didn't have his cell phone number, but I reached him at his desk at the Durham police headquarters.

Luke said they were following up on a theory that a gang called the M Street Crew was connected to the carjacking.

"We've arrested a suspect who had some blood spatter on him—if it's Jana's blood, that'll be enough to tie him to the carjacking," he said. "And if we're really lucky, her daughter, Shaina, will be able to identify him from a photo lineup."

An image of the window and Jana's head being shattered with a gun swam into my head.

Pushing the vision away, I said, "Shaina told

me she thinks her stepfather was behind it. And I heard that Jana left him two million dollars in life insurance."

I expected Luke to dismiss Shaina's suspicion about her stepfather the way Dr. Sanders had.

But he didn't. "We're looking into that," he said. "We know about Jana's insurance policy. But so far this case is looking like a straightforward carjacking, not a Black Widower job."

"But do you know about Gavin's first wife—that she died under suspicious circumstances?"

A pause. "Now, where did you hear *that*?" Luke asked me. "Did Jana or her daughter know about the first wife's death?"

"I don't think so. I just heard it from a source." I didn't want to say that Fish was my informant.

I heard Luke snort. "I know Jana hired Fish to help her with her divorce, Kate. It's not a big secret. Fish told me about it himself."

"Okay." At least he hadn't heard it from me.

"But don't believe everything you hear," Luke said in a reproving tone. "The police in Omaha looked at Gavin as a suspect, but her death was ultimately ruled *not* to be suspicious. And we didn't have to hear that from Fish. We're the homicide detectives, remember?"

"I know. Of course. But did you—"

"Don't worry, Kate. We're following up on all

the angles." Luke's tone was soothing but firm. "Trust me on this. Would you, please?"

His real meaning: Butt out.

I pulled into a parking space in the visitor's lot at Mercy Hospital. While I was locking the car, a Corvette with dealer plates pulled into the space next to me. The top was down, which gave me an unobstructed view of the couple inside. The driver had a reddish blow-over and one hand cupped around the breast of his flocculent blond companion. She was ignoring his hand as she reapplied lipstick in the visor mirror.

Even from several feet away I could smell the man's musky fragrance. It was so thick you'd think the guy had an electric aroma ball hung around his neck, with his hand plugged into Blondie's cleavage for power.

Get a room, why don't you? my love-bruised brain wanted to scream at the two of them. So surly were my thoughts right then that if I'd had my way, every lovey-dovey couple on earth would get an electric shock when they pressed their lips together.

When I passed the nurse's station on the fourth floor of the hospital, the nurse with the Caribbean accent recognized me.

"Oh, it's good that you're back now," she said

to me. "Our girl should be waking up any moment."

Inside Shaina's room, I sat on the visitor's chair and waited until her eyelids started to flutter.

"Shaina?" I asked as soon as she came to. "It's Kate here. Kate Gallagher."

"Mom's friend, right?" she said, blinking. "I remember you."

As I nodded, a nurse entered the room and started checking her vital signs.

Shaina shifted her gaze to the ceiling and lay quietly against the pillows. Her eyes were wide and tense looking, but they showed none of the hysteria that had been in them earlier in the day. The only emotion I could detect in them now was a weary anguish.

I touched her hand, and her eyes filled with tears. "I just can't believe I'm never going to hear my mother's voice again," she said. "It's not fair, Kate."

"I know," I replied. "It's not fair at all."

I desperately tried to think up some bromide, some reassuring words of comfort to offer to her. But I came up empty. Shaina had captured the stark, bitter truth—death was not fair.

Death had taken my own mother from me in a maliciously unfair way. It had happened on my thirteenth birthday.

"I'm on my way to get your cake, Katie. Back soon." Those had been my mother's final words to me that day. She'd blown an air kiss my way before turning away.

I don't even remember seeing her car leave the driveway of our South Boston duplex. I'd been too preoccupied putting the finishing touches on the decorations for my birthday party. I'd been planning the party for months—it was going to be a magic princess party. I'd asked all my girlfriends to dress up as their favorite characters. I was dressed as Xena, warrior princess, in a daring costume that my mother had sewed for me, complete with magic-power cuffs. I even had a plastic sword. I was sure that my costume was going to cause a stir among my friends, all of whom were planning to dress as Disney characters and fairy princesses.

Much of what happened the rest of that day was blanked out, covered over by a merciful, numbing blanket of severe emotional shock. I vaguely remember that my mother seemed to be taking a long time to pick up the cake. Then strangely, a procession of police cars had arrived—four of them pulled into our driveway, one behind the other. At the time I'd thought that my dad, who was captain of the sixth police district, had invited some of his officers to my birthday party.

I'd stepped out of the house only to be confronted by a ring of somber, drawn faces. Strangely, they'd all removed their hats. All they would say was that my dad was on his way home.

"Of course Dad's coming home," I said, looking around at them with a puzzled smile. "It's my birthday. My mom's bringing the cake."

The officers had shuffled their feet and looked down at the ground, saying nothing. Then my aunt Myra had arrived. Her face was crumpled. Behind her was another police car. This one had my father inside it. He was in the backseat, and his face was buried in his hands. It took me a moment to realize that my father was crying. I'd never seen him cry before.

Then my aunt Myra and my father pulled me into the living room. They gathered around me and wrapped me in their arms. I remember feeling confused and thinking that it felt like we were making a football huddle.

That's when they told me that my mother had been killed. I remember that I'd dropped my plastic sword—in that moment, it felt like the world was spinning. And as it spun, someone shoved a real blade through the middle of my heart. This one was made of steel.

The painful details would come later—my mother had walked in on an armed robbery at the bakery. The young punk had panicked; the gun had gone off; my mother was dead.

Looking at Shaina now, I knew that at that moment there could be no bromide, no words of comfort. For her the future would bring only a hard, unyielding sorrow.

Shaina had just suffered a wound that would never fully close. It would be in her heart forever. Perhaps someday her sorrow would be hidden beneath the surface of her everyday existence.

But it would always be there, as cold and deep as a grave.

Chapter 16

Avoid the Winter's Frost

If you are worried about aging eyes, steer clear of frosted eye shadows. Even a hint of frost emphasizes the wrinkles and creases above your eyes. A neutral, matte eye shadow is your best beauty choice.

—From *The Little Book of Beauty Secrets* by Mimi Morgan

I shook off the bleak thoughts about the loss of my mother and focused my attention on Shaina. Her face was tiny and pale, a porcelain doll's head lost in the middle of the hospital bedding. And terribly alone.

"Here's my uncle Belmont's phone number." Shaina wrote a number on a piece of paper I'd handed her. "The doctor told me that he and my aunt are flying back from the West Coast right now. They should be here in a couple of hours."

When I promised to get in touch with them, she peered into my face. "What have the police told you so far?"

"They'll talk to you when you're up to it," I said.

I didn't want to compromise anything the police were doing by saying too much to Shaina yet. Better for Luke to tell her what was going on. Any information she got from me risked influencing what she told the investigators about the attack.

Closing her eyes, Shaina leaned back against the pillows. "His face was young," she said. "And . . . this is going to sound weird, but he looked kind of scared. That doesn't make sense, does it? I didn't think he'd shoot her. I never even saw a gun. Why did he do it, Kate? There has to be a reason."

"These animals have their own reasons for killing," I said. "The reasons don't make sense to us. They're just thugs."

"I'm an orphan now," she said, as if testing out the sound of the unfamiliar word.

In a whisper she continued, "*Orphan.* That word sounds strange, doesn't it? When you're an orphan it seems like you should be a kid. Like Little Orphan Annie."

"It's a horrible thing to lose your parents no matter what age you are," I replied.

Shaina was staring past me. Then her neck arched back, and her gaze angled away at a guarded slant.

I turned around to see what she was looking away from.

A man charged into the room at a full-bore tilt. "My dear, how are you feeling?" he said. "Oh, my girl, I was thinking of you the entire drive up from Florida."

"Gavin." Shaina said the name in a flat-sounding voice. "Kate, this is my stepfather."

With a jolt, I recognized Gavin. He was the man I'd just seen outside in the parking garage. There was no mistaking the Trump-do and gaga-musky men's fragrance.

Jana's widower was Mr. Musk-and-Blow. Who, when last seen by me, had been playing hide-the-hand down the décolleté of the chesty blonde in his Corvette.

Chapter 17

Give Your Face an Instant Lift

*To brighten your face, run a light concealer or white
eyeliner from the top of your nose to your eyebrow,
and along the arch of your brow. You'll find it gives
your look an instant lift.*

—From *The Little Book of Beauty Secrets* by Mimi Morgan

Without thinking, I stepped between Gavin and
Shaina, blocking her stepfather's progress.

"What? Who are *you*?" Gavin said to me, taking a step back.

There was no glimmer of recognition in his
eyes. Obviously he'd been too wrapped up with
Miss Skanky Blonde to notice me standing right
next to his Corvette.

"I'm not up to seeing anyone right now,"
Shaina said to me.

Looking directly at her stepfather, she continued, "Please, Kate—can you make him go away?"

"Let's go outside for a moment," I said to
Gavin, hustling him out the door.

Once we were in the hallway, I closed the door to Shaina's room behind us.

"What's wrong with her?" Gavin sounded bewildered. "I drove here all the way from Florida to see her."

"Well, I'm sorry, but she said she's not up to seeing you right now. And anyway—don't you have someone waiting for you outside?"

Gavin shot me a guarded look. "What do you mean?" he demanded.

"I think you know what I'm talking about."

"It's not your business," he sputtered. "Like I said before, who the hell are *you*?"

"I'm a friend of Jana's. Your wife, remember? I saw you in your car out in the parking garage just a little while ago with that blonde. Isn't it inappropriate for you to bring your girlfriend with you to the hospital, right after your wife is killed?"

Gavin dug into his pocket and extracted his car keys, as if preparing to make a getaway. But it turned out he was just getting warmed up.

"I don't know what you think you saw," he said, his chest puffing up. "My assistant, Candice, drove up here with me from Miami. She's doing some work for me this week. That's all."

"Candice? You mean *Candy*, don't you? Admirer of the naked videos you sent her? I have sources who told me all about them, Gavin. Or is it Guido? Didn't you change your name?"

"What the— How *dare* you?"

Gavin swayed dangerously close. Even though it was before noon, I could smell whiskey on his breath.

A doctor passed by and scanned our tense body language with a curious expression.

As soon as the man was out of earshot, Gavin grabbed hold of my forearm. He wasn't a huge man, but his grip was painful.

"Who the *hell* do you think you are?" he said, lowering his voice to a growl. "You're interfering with my family's private business. You better back off, lady. I need to talk to my daughter."

"Shaina's your *step*daughter, remember? And right now she doesn't want to talk to you."

"That's enough. I'm having you thrown out."

"That'd be great. In fact, why don't you call the police, Gavin? You make out with a girlfriend at the hospital the day your wife is murdered? I'm sure they'll be interested to hear about that."

"The police will be *quite* interested, in fact."

Luke was standing next to me in the hallway. I hadn't heard him approach. Neither had Gavin, apparently, from the startled look he gave the detective.

Next to Luke was a cop I'd never seen before.

He must have recently been promoted to detective grade, or else his wife had just given him a makeover; his blazer-and-khakis outfit looked fresh off the rack. Every movement seemed slightly uncomfortable.

Luke opened his wallet and showed his badge to Gavin.

"You're Gavin Spellmore, husband of Jana Miller?"

When Gavin nodded, he continued, "I'm Detective Luke Petronella of Durham Homicide. I'd like you to chat for a few moments with my colleague Detective Stripling."

Gavin opened his mouth as if to protest, then closed it again.

Grabbing me by an elbow, Luke spun me away from Gavin and herded me down the hallway.

I expected Luke to pump me for information about what I'd learned about the tête-à-tête I'd seen between Gavin and his girlfriend in the Corvette. But Luke surprised me by scowling. At *me*.

"What the hell were you doing just now, Kate?" he asked. "You haven't been talking to my witness Shaina about this case, have you?"

"Of course not," I said. "But I just saw her stepfather, Gavin, outside playing a game of booby trap with his girlfriend. That's why Jana was divorcing him. Doesn't that make him a likely suspect in her murder?"

"Oh, so now you're a historian for the War of the Roses. Are you planning to go to detective school, too?"

Before I could reply, he kept on blasting, "Are you *shittin'* me, Kate? If you screw up my case, I will poach both your ass cheeks and serve them up cold on an English muffin for breakfast. With bacon."

"I have no idea what that's supposed to mean, Luke, but you don't have to threaten me."

"I wouldn't have thought of threatening you before now. After witnessing this little hallway performance of yours, I may have to change my mind."

He stabbed the air with a commanding finger. "Remember, Kate," he said. "Your bacon. *In* the eggs Benedict."

I rolled my eyes. Luke loves food metaphors, but he always messes them up.

I mean, everyone *knows* that eggs Benedict doesn't come with bacon.

Chapter 18

God's Gift to Women on the Beach

If you're worried about baring your hips and thighs on the beach this summer, I've got two words to whisper to you: board shorts.

All you have to do is pair some board shorts with a maillot top, and you've got the ingredients for a swimsuit solution that will overcome—or at least cover up—most figure flaws.

—From *The Little Book of Beauty Secrets* by Mimi Morgan

On the way home from the hospital, I reached Shaina's uncle Belmont Miller by telephone. The Millers had just landed at RDU Airport from Los Angeles in—must be nice—their private Gulfstream jet.

"I owe you one for keeping that jerk Gavin away from Shaina," Belmont said when I told him what had happened at the hospital. "He's the *last* person she should see right now. I wonder why he was so insistent on seeing her."

The possible answer made me shudder. What

if Shaina was right and Gavin had had Jana killed? What if he'd had her mother murdered for the insurance money? The notion seemed far-fetched, but I wasn't in the mood to overlook any possibilities.

As I was mulling that over, Belmont continued, "We're going to take Shaina to our cottage in the Bahamas. She can recover there."

"So soon?"

"The doctors said she's okay to travel. I just got off the line with the police. I gather from the detectives that they've already gotten all the information they need from her for now. We'll fly her back in for anything else they need."

"Still, I don't know if it's best that she—"

"I've brought our private physician with us. Don't worry—Shaina will get the best of care." All at once, Belmont sounded like he was in a hurry to end the conversation.

I wasn't too happy about the idea that Shaina was going to be whisked out of the country right after her mother's death. It was hard to wrap my head around the idea of bopping around the world on a private jet with one's own doctor. It sounded like the life of royals. Even though I'd always known Jana came from a rich family, I'd never realized *how* rich.

Belmont, Luke—everyone, it seemed—were

telling me not to worry, that things were under control. They had their suspect and their story lines straight. But I still had a duty to my friend Jana.

I needed to know *why* she'd been killed.

Chapter 19

Protect Against Sun Damage
with Tea Tree Oil Products

Here's a hint from my dermatologist: Products with tea tree oil will help protect your skin against most of the sun damage that sneaks past the protection of your sunscreen.

—From *The Little Book of Beauty Secrets* by Mimi Morgan

The clouds cleared away that afternoon just in time for the Newbodies to hold the Memory Ceremony for Jana.

At four p.m. I was clutching the prickly stem of a red rose in my right hand, a white rose in my left—red to symbolize life, white for death.

Eight women were clustered around me atop a stone bridge that spanned New Hope Creek in Duke Forest. The rains had transformed the boulder-pocked rivulet into muddy rapids; all around us was the sound of rushing water and the smell of damp earth.

Frank crouched below us at the shoreline, his camera resting on his shoulder. Bringing a crew along had actually been Evelyn's idea. I'd resisted at first, not wanting to exploit Jana's death. But Evelyn had already text-polled the Newbodies, and all eight women had decided unanimously that broadcasting the ceremony would provide a highway to release Jana's spirit to the cosmos.

The only member who hadn't made it to the gathering was Trish Putnam, who was still out of town. I'd left her a message on her cell about Jana, but had missed her return call. I still wanted to find out what had become of Jana's purse, which she'd left at Trish's house on the night of the Newbodies meeting. I'd have to follow up about that with her later.

Evelyn stood at the crest of the bridge, facing us. She was wearing a full-length white dress and carrying a woven basket. The basket had pieces of paper in it.

"As you all know, Jana Miller was a former member of the Newbodies," Evelyn began. "She moved away to Miami a couple of years ago but kept in close touch and was a good friend to many of us. We've come here today to honor her life with our spirit memories."

Evelyn started handing out pieces of paper and tiny pencils from the basket.

As she distributed the items to each of us, she continued, "This is biodegradable paper that will dissolve almost instantly and leave no pollution in the creek," she said. "I'd like us each to write a spiritual memory of Jana. Then we'll release the notes and the roses into the water."

When I got my piece of paper, I stared at it for a while, unsure what a "spiritual memory" was. Then I knew.

Jana, I wrote. *Shaina is fine and she misses you very much. The police have made an arrest. I'll keep following up until I'm satisfied they have the right person. I hope you're at peace now. Love, Kate.*

It was an oddly factual, unspiritual message.

But hey, I'm a reporter, not a psychic.

And if by some miracle my message managed to reach Jana on the other side of life, I hoped she'd appreciate the update.

Chapter 20

Brighten Those Red Eyes

You can brighten tired-looking red eyes. Simply line the inside of the lower lid with white pencil—this has the effect of brightening the whites of your eyes.

—From *The Little Book of Beauty Secrets* by Mimi Morgan

Our after-ceremony was much less spiritual than the Memory Ceremony had been.

At my suggestion, a few of us met at Bugtussles. By now it was seven p.m., and I was in serious need of decompression, one involving libation and perhaps some of Bartender Bernie's famous hamburger sliders.

Four of us made the pilgrimage—me, Evelyn, and two women I'd first met at the Tuesday night Newbodies meeting.

Passersby were shooting curious glances at us. We were at the bar, but we certainly weren't in bar-chat mode.

Evelyn was still wearing her Sister Aimee

gown, with roses in her hair that she'd picked up at the Memory Ceremony.

"We don't have a quorum here to decide anything tonight," she said. "But I'm thinking we should probably disband the Newbodies."

"Don't we need to talk to Trish about that before even *discussing* it?" said Monique, a shockingly tall woman who had the most over-developed neck I'd ever seen. "I don't want to preempt."

Monique had once been named Michael, I'd heard, which probably explained the height *and* the neck.

"Certainly I don't mean to preempt Trish," Evelyn said in a defensive tone. "But I'm scared. Too much has happened. Like what about the fact that Anaïs Loring was killed last spring? Who's next?"

Celia, who had a pasty-white complexion that made her look like she'd been bitten by a vampire, looked up from her drink. "You didn't even know Anaïs, Evelyn," she said. "I did, and I certainly can't imagine any possible connection between Anaïs and Jana. Let's all take a deep breath and not overreact."

Trust a vampire to stay calm.

What calmed *me* was the timely arrival of the platter of hamburger sliders.

"Back when Anaïs was killed during the robbery, what did the police say about it?" I asked Celia, popping a slider into my mouth.

"Not very much," Celia said. "They talked to everyone in the Newbodies at the time. I don't know if they talked to Jana, though, because she was in Miami."

After a pause she added, "Actually, I kind of got the sense that I was being questioned a bit about Anaïs's murder. Did you get that sense, Monique?"

Monique looked stricken. "You mean, like as a *suspect*? Not at all," she said. "They just asked who'd been at Anaïs's house around the time of the murder. And of course we'd all been there for the Newbodies meeting. That's all."

With a shrug Celia said, "Well, they needed to know exactly where I was when the robbery took place. I remember they said Anaïs was killed at ten p.m. But maybe they only did me that way. I've never gotten along with cops—they're *always* writing me tickets."

Monique checked in with her watch.

"Oh, darn," she said, reaching for her purse. "I forgot I told my roommate I'd walk her stupid dog tonight. He's probably peed all over the place by now. Will twenty cover my drink?"

"It'll more than cover it," I said. "Hang on, Monique; I'll give you your—"

But Monique had already left the building.

Early Friday morning, I drove directly to Durham police headquarters. I wanted to talk to Luke some more about Jana's murder, but from the way he'd freaked out at me at the hospital, I knew I'd better have a good strategy.

The operator at the Durham Police Department told me that Luke was in an "official meeting." That was squad jargon that detectives used when they didn't want to be hassled by the phone, Jonathan had once told me. So I decided to walk into his office unannounced.

On the way over, I picked up a latte and a bagel with cream cheese at a deli. Not exactly what you'd call a healthy start to the day, but I gave myself brownie points for rejecting the apple fritter, which had a thick layer of glaze and must've packed a gazillion calories.

The silhouette of the Durham police headquarters squatted beneath a sky the color of cinderblocks. Inside the main lobby, Tanya, the desk sergeant, nodded to me through the ancient Plexiglas divider.

"Working on something here today, Kate?"

"Yeah, Tanya, I'm here to do a little research

in ballistics. Okay if I just wander around a bit?"

"Sure thing."

I'm the only reporter Tanya lets roam the hallways of headquarters without an escort. She and I had forged an early bond after we discovered that we were both avid shoppers of plus-sized clothing. Sergeant Tanya's got "back" as the saying goes. She jokes that her butt pushes her police trousers far beyond the call of duty. We've been buddies ever since I told her about Sassy D's, an online treasure trove for women who have more to love. The other reporters never could figure out why I have such pull with Tanya. I call it the Sisterhood of the Plus-Sized Pants.

"You should check out that sale at Sassy's this week," Tanya whispered after buzzing me through the door. "I just bought their last pair of fence-net hose in a size double-X."

"*Fence*-net hose?"

"Yeah," she said with a smile that showed a slight gap between her front teeth. "It helps me fence in my boyfriend, Hugo."

"I could use some fencing right now when it comes to my love life," I said, signing the registry sheet. "My boyfriend seems to have kicked down the corral posts."

Oops. I hadn't meant to refer to Jonathan at his place of work. My bad.

Inside the detective's bureau room I shot an involuntary glance at Jonathan's empty desk. Its surface was neat and organized—amazingly clean, as if he'd sprayed it with disinfectant before leaving. Not a single personal picture was on the surface, including none of me, I noted. His desk looked like it belonged to someone who might not be coming back.

Luke's desk, on the other hand, was strewn with personal tokens and other artifacts—family pictures, file folders in various colors, plus an ancient, crumpled brown bag.

Luke looked up from his reports. He gave me a flinty-eyed cop stare.

"I've got to tell Tanya to start doing her job better and swat away fruit flies like you at the door," he said.

"Catch," he said, tossing me a tangerine.

I caught it one-handed. "Thanks."

I wasn't hungry after my bagel. But I knew better than to reject Luke's peace offering.

While I peeled the tangerine, an awkward silence fell between us. Normally one of us would have filled the gap with a mention of Jonathan. The fact that we didn't meant that something strange was going on. Jonathan had become an unmentionable elephant in the room.

To break the pall I said, "So what happened after I left the hospital? With Jana's husband, I mean?"

When Luke hesitated, I rolled my eyes. "And I know I don't have to mention that we're off the record right now."

"Right," he said. "But seeing how you're a reporter, I know I've got to watch my ass around you. If anything off the record goes on the air, you're shit on my shoe—you got that? I'm only talking to you at all because you're a friend of Jana's. And because you're *my* friend, kind of. When I'm not having to scrape you off my heel, that is."

"Consider me scraped."

Luke spread open the red file folder in front of him.

Red files, I knew, were used for open homicides; cold cases went into blue folders; closed cases were sent to the archives.

"We interviewed Jana's husband," Luke said. He's got a solid-sounding alibi. "There's nothing at all to implicate the guy in her murder. Nothing at all."

"What about the fact that he had his hand down his girlfriend's blouse in the hospital's parking garage? And the fact that Jana was divorcing him and that he gets nada much unless she's dead? That's not solid enough to implicate him for you?"

"We're considering all of that. I'm just saying

that so far, Jana Miller's death has gone by the numbers."

He peered down at his notes in the file and made an exasperated gargling noise in the back of his throat.

"Strip!" he projected in a booming voice. "Does the—"

"Jesus Christ, Luke."

Detective Stripling's head rose above the other side of a filing cabinet. He had one fist wrapped around the unwrapped portion of an energy bar. Stripling nodded at me, then used the bar to make a rude gesture at Luke.

"I'm right over here eating a snack where I always am," he said. "How many times do I have to tell you that you don't have to scream?"

"Sure I do," Luke replied. "Normal people can't tell when you've got those damned music plugs in your ears. Is Jana Miller's family insisting on doing a private autopsy?"

"I couldn't talk 'em out of it. I told her brother and their lawyer that it would be a waste of their ample money. They wouldn't listen."

When Stripling's head vanished behind the filing cabinet again, Luke looked at me.

"'Waste of time' is right. Our medical examiner's office is the best in the state. And the cause of death is straightforward in Jana's case. Two gunshots to the head. But we'll give them the corpse if they insist.

"Sorry," he added, after I flinched at the term "corpse" in reference to my friend.

"What will be they be looking for specifically, do you know?" I asked him.

"They'll be looking for anything that proves we don't know how to do our jobs or that we screwed up," Luke said with a shrug. "Rich people. What are you gonna do? They think only the private sector knows how to do anything right."

"Have you gotten a confession from your suspect?"

"Nah. That scumbag lawyered up real fast. He hired himself a pretty good one, too. That was actually kind of surprising. Usually these assholes can only afford public defenders."

"Maybe someone else is paying for the lawyer," I suggested. "Maybe the person who is really behind Jana's murder is footing the tab."

"Well, aren't you a regular little CSI. Were you thinking it was someone like Gavin Spellmore, Jana's husband?"

When I gave a quick nod, Luke leaned back in his chair. "Jesus Christ, Kate, would you give it a rest? Jonathan told me you lock onto a point like a pit bull and don't let go, but I'm telling you that you're probably wrong in this case. Okay?"

Like a *pit bull*? Yee-ouch.

My cheeks burst into flame. "Certainly I could be wrong," I said. "But you haven't convinced me yet."

"Well, you're not the friggin' district attorney that I have to convince, now, are you?"

Slapping the file shut, he continued, "Anyway, Shaina has already ID'd our suspect—Antoine Hurley. She picked him out of a photo lineup after you left the hospital."

"Shaina identified Antoine Hurley as the carjacker?"

"Isn't that what I just said? I believe I did."

"Yes, but what about the shooting? Shaina didn't see a gun, she told me. And besides—even if Antoine shot Jana, he might have been hired by someone else. By Jana's husband, Gavin, for example. Have you considered that?"

"Of course. And have *you* considered that having a lousy marriage and a girlfriend on the side doesn't mean a guy had his wife killed?"

"It doesn't mean he *didn't* have her killed, either."

Luke was grinning now. He was having fun. "You'd never make a real cop, you know," he said. "You're like one of those UFO conspiracy guys. You'd waste all the taxpayers' money trying to disprove a theory that's all in your head.

Like did we *really* land on the moon? That's for *The X Files* and nut jobs."

"I'm not even going to dignify that," I replied with a sniff. "Jana told me Gavin was stealing from her right before she died. To the tune of tens of thousands of dollars. And Fish told me—"

Luke lifted his palms in the air like a preacher beseeching the heavens. Then he pointed at me. "I already told you, Kate—*former* Detective Fisher is a drunk and a psych case. So you can take all his information with a friggin' dump-truck-load of salt. Okay?"

Glancing away, he added, "As for Gavin Spellmore, well . . . look. Plenty of guys have something going on outside their marriage, or maybe they raid the family's piggy bank. That's just the way some men are."

"Oh, shit, Luke. That's just a rationalization, and you know it. How can you sit there and *defend* the guy when you know that he—"

"Look. I'm not defending this rat fucker," he said. "But having an affair doesn't make the guy a wife murderer. If that were true, we'd have to arrest half the male population in the United States. Hell, we'd have to arrest half the guys in this room. Why do you think it's called the dick squad?"

"Shut up, Luke," a disembodied voice announced.

Someone chucked an apple core across the room. The pippin projectile sailed past my nose, headed for Luke.

While Luke ducked out of the way, I shot another glance at Jonathan's desk. When Luke had talked about men having affairs, it felt as if he was talking about me and Jonathan directly. Plus, now I knew that Jonathan had called me a pit bull to his coworkers. It wasn't exactly what you'd call a term of endearment. Would someone who loved you call you a pit bull to his coworkers? I don't think so.

I wondered whether Luke or any of Jonathan's friends in the United States knew about Gi. Probably not. Jonathan usually kept his personal matters close to the chest.

But maybe he'd kept Gi secret only from me. Maybe everyone else in town knew about her, and I was a laughingstock. The thought made the tangerine I'd just eaten start fizzing in my stomach.

Was I Jonathan's "something on the side"? Just a little something to be disposed of the minute his wife insinuated her size-zero butt back into the picture? Was that what I was when you broke it down? Jonathan's naive, stupid fool. That's exactly it.

I sat for a moment longer, trying to dismiss the distraction of having my head planted firmly up my ass. Then a new thought struck me.

"I forgot to tell you about something," I said to Luke. "It's about Jana's purse."

"What purse?"

"Jana's Miu Miu bag. When Jana and I had lunch on Wednesday, she said she thought she'd left it at a friend's house the night before. She was going to try to get it back."

Luke reached for a notepad and pen from his desk and started making notes.

"Name of friend with Jana's moo-moo . . . um, purse?"

"Trish Putnam. I don't know whether Jana got it back before she was killed."

"And what was Jana doing over at the Putnam home that night?"

"She was there for a support group. I was there, too. It's a women's group called the New-bodies."

"New *what*?"

"Newbodies. It's a body-image support group. They—"

"I don't give a shit what it is. Tell me about the purse."

"It was a bronze metallic color. By the de-signer Miu Miu."

Luke started leafing through Jana's file. "*Strip!* Check with Inventory to see if a brown purse was found in the Miller car. Had cows on it or some kind of shit like that."

Strip's voice said, "There wasn't a purse in the car. We assumed it was jacked during the attack on the women."

"You *assumed*?" Luke rolled his eyes. "Well, right now it's apparently sitting at some lady's house. Not jacked. And you call yourself a detective? Cripes almighty."

While Luke continued making notes, I said, "Here's something else interesting, Luke—the woman who founded the Newbodies group was killed last spring in a home-invasion robbery. Her name was Anaïs Loring. Evidently the detectives in that case talked to some of the members of the Newbodies group at the time. That's an odd coincidence, huh? I heard her murder is unsolved, by the way."

"And of course you were thinking I should pull up that other woman's murder file," Luke said without looking up from his notes. "You know, most pains in the ass aren't as cute and charming as you, Kate. That's your secret weapon."

He tossed the pen on top of the notepad, then leaned back in his chair. "But I can tell you right now that a cold-case murder in a ladies' social club probably won't pan out into anything," he said, cracking his knuckles. "I'll pull the Anaïs Loring file, but these two deaths have got *coincidence* written all over them. Besides. We have our prime suspect in jail. Antoine Hurley."

That was fine by me. Even if Anaïs Loring's death wound up as nothing more than an investigator's footnote in Jana's file, at least I'd have the satisfaction of knowing that I'd kicked over every stone.

Including the ones that the "real" investigators were ready to ignore.

Chapter 21

Lashes to Die For

Are you lusting for long, thick eyelashes? Just follow these simple rules when applying your mascara:

- *Keep your wand fresh—be sure to replace your mascara every few months. Nothing flakes and cakes like old, past-its-prime mascara.*
- *Curl your lashes with a good lash curler (I recommend Shimura's). Start by curling them at the base of the lashes, and then gently move the curling wand toward the end of the lashes, curling gently as you go.*

—From *The Little Book of Beauty Secrets* by Mimi Morgan

Saturday morning I came groggily awake to the pile-driving beat of the alarm clock. I tried to escape by burying my head under a pillow, but then something began dragging a strip of sandpaper along the back of my hand. It was Elfie. Evidently she'd decided that I was in need of a cat bath, or maybe she was simply trying to see whether I was still alive.

"Hey there, kitty," I croaked.

What I really needed was a hot shower. Surrounding me was the detritus of a blowout binge from the night before—Snickers wrappers, an empty pint of Pralines 'n' Cream, foil crumpoids of chocolate kisses—I'd spent the previous night in the sweet embrace of one of my worst sugar benders so far of the autumn. And it wasn't even Halloween yet.

I struggled to open my eyes and found them glued together by sleep crystals that had formed overnight. That always happened in the wake of a massive intake of chocolate and high-fructose corn syrup. Let the Hollywood celebrities risk their lives with prescription drugs and worse. I preferred to take the edge off pain with pure, unadulterated sugar. If only I didn't pay for my sins in poundage the next day. That was the killer.

I pried open my eyes with my fingers, then checked the messages on my cell phone. Four of the messages were from Jonathan.

"Oh, sure. *Now* you want to talk." A surge of anger flowed through my fingers. I autodeleted Jonathan's messages without listening to them. Let him worry about what *I* was thinking for once.

In the wake of that feeble act of payback, the silence felt hollow. What had Jonathan wanted to say to me? What *was* there to say? He was married. Or at the very least, he had slept with his ex-wife. End of story.

After checking on Shaina—the head nurse informed me that she was going to be released later that day—I made a pot of coffee and toasted a bagel. I wound up ignoring the bagel. The eating frenzy of the night before had left me feeling stuffed. Sick, even.

I stepped on the bathroom scale. Despite my binge of the night before, I'd lost two pounds since the previous weekend, but even that news didn't lift my spirits.

The Broken Heart Diet—boffo idea for a best-selling diet book, I thought with grim satisfaction. *The cover will display a red heart, and your lover's ex-wife will be driving a fork through it. And the ex-wife's name will be Gi.*

The only thing that could make the moment worse would be to get a call I'd been avoiding all week.

Right on schedule, the phone rang.

"Have you been watching CNN?" My father's voice came booming over the line.

"Not today, Dad."

"I don't want to tell you your business, Kate," Dad said. "But CNN just ran a story about the possibility of earthquakes on the East Coast. Very close to where you are, in fact. Did you know that all the original homes in Charleston were built with earthquake bolts?"

"I didn't know that," I said. "But actually, Charleston's not all that close to Durham. Different state. That's South Carolina."

"Still, it's next door to you. And they had a huge shaker in 1866. I'm thinking that the entire Southeast needs to prepare for a major eight-point shaker. Your viewers should know about it. Do you have your earthquake kit prepared?"

"Uh, no."

"That's what I thought. I'm sending you one in the mail. It includes a windup solar radio. This way you'll never be without a radio if the electricity goes out."

Ever since he'd retired from his job as police captain, Dad had found a new career keeping me posted on every twist and turn of the national—and even international—news. He seemed to think that if there was any news breaking anywhere in the world, I needed to know about it instantly. He never seemed to quite distinguish—or care—about the lines that divide local, national, and international news. Every few months he asked me why he couldn't see me on cable in Boston. It drove me batty.

"Well, thanks, Dad. I'll—"

"Before I let you go, I want to know—have you had your blood pressure checked recently?"

"Yes. I had it checked at the pharmacy."

"You know, you can't rely on those pharmacy cuffs. You need to have your pressure taken by a qualified physician. Preferably by a cardiologist."

"A *cardiologist*? Dad, I'm only twenty-seven years old."

"It's never too soon to start tracking your health baselines. High blood pressure and stroke run in our family, you know."

"I know. Okay, Dad, thanks."

My dad had always been a worrywart about me, but recently his concern had gone off the Richter scale. A week didn't go by when he didn't mail me a copy of an article warning about some kind of potential disaster.

I was beginning to think it was time to try to get my dad set up with a lady friend, just for the distraction factor. In fact, I'd e-mailed him some links to articles about how to troll the romantic waters on the Internet. With his silver-haired good looks and "command presence," as they called it in the police world, my dad would be a surefire hit on Internet matchmaking services like eHarmony.com. But my dad claimed to have no interest in dating—no one could ever rival my mother in his eyes, he always said.

Meanwhile, Dad must have homed in on something he'd heard in my voice. "You sound like you're under stress," he said. "What's going on? What's wrong?"

"Nothing's wrong," I said in a guarded tone.

"Yes, there is, but I know you won't tell me. Well, I'm putting something else in the mail for you. Maybe it'll help with whatever's worrying you."

"Nothing's worrying me. What are you sending?"

"Just a little something for your personal protection. It's high time you graduated from that pocketknife you carry around on your keychain. I've been telling you that for years."

"It's not a gun, is it?" I asked, wincing. "Because you know I won't carry a firearm."

"Of course not. And anyway, sending a gun through the mail would violate federal regulations."

What a relief. The Second Amendment is my dad's favorite passage in the Constitution. In his opinion Switzerland—a nation with an unusually high per capita gun ownership rate—has the right idea for preventing crime.

Blow off their buns when they come through your

door and they won't come back is one of his favorite sayings.

"What are you sending, then?" I asked.

"You'll just have to wait and see, won't you?"

Next, I set off on a sad mission.

Trish had left a message letting me know that I could pick up Jana's purse from her house. Trish and her husband were still out of town, but she said her son would be at the house to give me the purse.

I'd never heard anything back from Luke about Jana's purse. Maybe he didn't think the purse was relevant to the case against their murder suspect, Antoine Hurley. So I guessed it was okay if I went ahead and picked it up. Luke had made it abundantly clear that he thought I obsessed about minor details. Maybe you didn't do that if you were a homicide detective.

In the midmorning light, Trish's sprawling colonial home was larger and even more impressive than I remembered from the Newbodies meeting on Tuesday night.

When I rang the front doorbell, no one answered for a long while. I rang a couple more times before hearing a stirring deep within.

Chaz Putnam opened the door. He was wear-

ing the same flannel shirt he'd had on the night
of the Newbodies party. The shirt was even
grimier than it had been on Tuesday night.

Chaz stood framed in the doorway, swaying
slightly.

"Kate Gallagher, right?" he said.

When I nodded, he made a low, sweeping
bow. "Channel Twelve News," he said. "I'm *hon-
ored*."

The treacly-herbal smell I remembered from
the other night was rolling off him in waves
again. Pot. It was only ten a.m.—even for a young
slacker that seemed early to be flying high.

"Are you okay, Chaz?" I asked him.

"*Oh*, yeah." Raising two fingers to his lips as if
he were taking a hit off a joint, he said, "Nothing
like a morning drag to take the edge off. But don't
tell my mom, okay?"

When I shrugged, he grinned. "C'mon in,
then," he said. "The purse is in the kitchen."

I followed Chaz into the Putnams' kitchen,
which turned out to be larger than my entire
apartment. Jana's bag was resting on top of a
round table in a breakfast nook.

We stood silently for a moment, staring at the
purse. It looked unspeakably sad all by itself in
the middle of the clean white table.

"I heard about what happened to that lady,"
Chaz said, shooting a sideways glance at me.

"That was too bad. But they caught the guy who did it, right?"

"So the police say."

I started to reach for the bag, then hesitated. "By the way," I said. "Have the homicide detectives called here asking about this purse?"

"Have the police called *here*?" Underneath a layer of stubble, Chaz's skin turned ashen. "No. Why would they?"

"I told the detective in charge of the investigation that Jana left it here the night of your mom's meeting," I said. "I was just wondering whether they wanted to pick it up themselves." Reaching for my cell phone, I added, "I'll just call them to check before I take it."

Before my fingers could touch the keypad, I felt a sharp blow on my wrist.

The cell phone dropped from my hand and went spinning across the kitchen's hardwood floor.

Chapter 22

Keep the Raccoons Away

Be sure to visit the ladies' room every few hours to clean up any mascara or liner that migrates during the day. Use a no-oil mascara remover and a cotton swab to whisk away any fledgling raccoon eyes.

—From *The Little Book of Beauty Secrets* by Mimi Morgan

"Are you out of your *mind*?" Chaz's eyes loomed large and spooky looking in my face as he asked the question—he must have knocked the cell phone out of my hand.

Without waiting for a reply, he hissed, "I've got pot and servers in my room. And you want to bring cops over *here*?"

I rubbed my wrist, which hurt like hell. He must've hit me with one heck of a blow. It seemed like an overreaction.

"Jesus Christ, Chaz," I said. "I was calling homicide detectives, not the narcs. They're conducting a murder investigation. They're not looking for pot or a couple of bongs in your room. Is that what you mean by 'servers'?"

"No," he said, his tone exasperated. "Servers are computers."

"Oh, right," I said, feeling like a Luddite. "Why are you worried about the police seeing your computers?"

"I'm not, but I certainly don't need cops poking their noses in my business right now. The second you let them in, all hell can break loose."

Thrusting Jana's purse at me, he said, "Just take this stupid hag bag and go away."

He was shaking; sweat was trickling down from his temples toward his chin. He looked like someone who could easily launch into another attack at any second.

I picked up my phone from the floor. Carefully sliding it into my pants pocket, I kept my gaze focused on Chaz.

"No problem, Chaz," I said.

Hugging Jana's purse close to me, I wheeled around.

Then I left as fast as I could.

After leaving the Putnam house, I spent the rest of the morning at the Channel Twelve studios. Things there got off to a rip-roaring start with a Lainey encounter.

The instant I set foot inside the newsroom, Lainey planted herself in front of me, armed with her trademark faux-friendly smile. She wore her blond hair curved off her face in a power lift; somehow it managed to stay aloft without visible bobby pinnage.

"Hi, Kate. Let's talk," she said, touching my arm.

"What is it, Lainey?"

"I'm supposed to work with Frank today," she said. "But for some reason, he's assigned to you on the whiteboard." Lainey's tone made it sound as if I'd swiped her PowerBar.

Glancing up at the assignment board, I saw Frank's name written next to mine. In two hours we were supposed to shoot the first installment of my series about weight-loss scams—the dreaded bikini story. And here I was, still bikiniless.

"Right you are. And actually I'm running behind, so I'm busy right now," I said, trying to step around her.

Lainey leaned in to block me. "Frank's the most experienced videographer for police rollouts, so I need him," she said. "We're going on a ride-along with the gang patrol—I've got it all set up. It's hard news."

Frank, who had his butt parked against the assignment desk, was pretending to check through his camera bag. He knew better than to get between two reporters who were fighting over him.

"Oh, you're doing hard news?" I feigned an impressed expression. "In that case, I think you should take Frank for the whole day. After all, we're talking about a *big* story, right?"

Plucking a purple marker from my purse, I handed it to her and nodded toward the whiteboard. "Go ahead and put your name up," I said.

Lainey's head of steam seemed to evaporate.

"Fine, then," she said with a toss of her head. "Thanks *so* much, Kate."

Marching over to the board, she crossed Frank's name off my story. She used the marker to write in his name next to hers, then did a victory march to her cubicle. Thankfully her desk was on the opposite end of the newsroom from mine.

Nearby, I heard the irritable slap of a newspaper against a desk. That meant that Tucker, the weekend producer, had arrived for work.

I knew that Tucker was no fan of Lainey's because of the way she threw fits every time she had to do any work that didn't feature her mug on camera. This seemed like an auspicious moment to bid him a casual good morning.

"Hey, Tucker," I said, lowering my voice. "Just FYI, we need to find a new videographer for my diet story installment today. Lainey said she needs Frank to work with her all afternoon."

"Oh, she *did*, did she?" Tucker scanned the whiteboard with an irritated look. "Hmph."

Reaching for an eraser, he added, "Certain people need to learn that *management* makes the assignments, not reporters."

He paused midswipe. "Who the hell used purple marker on the whiteboard? *Permanent* marker?" he bellowed. "Lanston!"

The reporters who'd been idling around the newsroom dove for cover.

Slowly, above the cubicle line, Lainey's streaked updo rose into view. Underneath her airbrushed war paint, her cheeks glowed a bright tangerine orange. It was like watching the arrival of the Great Pumpkin.

Frank, who hadn't glanced up from his gear during the entire exchange, chuckled under his breath. "Score one for Girl Gallagher."

I could feel Lainey's glare burning Swiss-cheese holes through me as I headed to my desk. But for the first time in a long, long while, the pressure felt good. I had a minor but heady sense of victory over my newsroom rival. Okay, so maybe the marker thing was petty, but it felt great to scuff up that golden halo of hers a little bit.

A bright pink box was sitting on top of my desk. It had a note taped to it:

Kate,
    Try this on. It did wonders for Kirstie's Big
Reveal on the Oprah show. Break a leg!
Love,
Evelyn
P.S. Open this in the ladies' room.

Following Evelyn's advice, I retreated to a stall in the restroom. Folded inside the box in layers of tissue was a ruby red bikini.

Hastily, I stripped off my slacks and top. Then I pulled on the suit. The halter top and high-cut bottoms were stretchy. They felt actually . . . okay.

Taking a deep breath, I stepped out and took a look at myself in the mirror. The halter top was spectacular, and the merlot-colored garment complemented my skin tone and hair perfectly. But there was no camouflaging my stomach.

"Thanks for trying, Evelyn," I said aloud. "But I'm doomed."

Something else was resting at the bottom of the box, wrapped carefully in tissue. I unwrapped it and held it at arm's length. It was a sheer, almost invisible garment.

It took me a moment to realize what I was looking at. It was a full-length, nylon body stocking. The label said, STRIPPER HOSE BY SAMANTHA.

I took the swimsuit back off and pulled the

thin, gossamer film over my body. It was like donning a second skin—all the cellulite dimples in my stomach and upper thigh bulges were instantly smoothed out.

Next, I put on the bikini. With the almost-invisible body stocking, my stomach looked flat, held in. And best of all, the camera would never be the wiser. It would look to the viewing audience like I wasn't wearing anything at all.

I ran my hands over my abdomen and thighs. Hallelujah . . . I might still be a plus-sized woman, but thanks to the miracle of stripper-illusion technology, there was reason to celebrate. From the right angle I could pass for one of those cha-cha cherubs from the Renaissance era. Heck, give me some pink chiffon and a grotto and I'd be ready to rumba with the Three Graces.

Now if only a master artist like old Peter Paul Rubens were still around to show me how to paint my fat-scam series by the numbers, I might not be so nervous.

Chapter 23

A Word to the Wise about Body Wraps

Body wraps (where you get wrapped in bandages that are soaked in mineral clay) can help you lose inches. Here's the bad news—it's all water loss. Some salons claim that their wraps can zap away cellulite, but there's no medical data to support that.

If you're in the mood for some temporary tightening, however, you might want to try a body wrap.

—From *The Little Book of Beauty Secrets* by Mimi Morgan

Two hours later I was laid out on a table at a salon called Skinny Wraps. My body was wrapped from neck to toe in white bandage strips soaked in mineral clay. I looked like an escapee from *Revenge of the Chubby Mummy*.

"So, where's your escape camel, Kate? Cooling its toes outside the pyramid?" Frank called out. He was crouched in the corner of the room with his camera, getting a low-angle shot of me getting plaster-cast in a body wrap.

"You're a funny guy, Frankenstein. Kiss my Irish ass."

"You want to see funny, wait till you get a load of this shot on camera." Frank moved in for a tight-in of my mummified thighs—my punishment for calling him by his most-hated nickname, Frankenstein.

A "reduction technician" named Yolanda took my measurements with a tape measure. For this part of the show, I'd donned my bikini. Even though my measurements were embarrassing, at least the surfaces were smooth and tight, thanks to Evelyn's stripper stocking. God bless her.

"We have an excellent result," Yolanda announced in a German-sounding accent that turned *W*s into *V*s. "You've lost eleven inches total from your body measurements."

Since I'd started with about two *hundred* inches total (counting practically every curved surface on my body), that was a five percent shrinkage. And even though I suspected that Yolanda might have taken some slight liberties with the tape measure to shave off some inches, secretly I was impressed.

Overall, the taping at Skinny Wraps had gone much better than I'd expected. That was a good thing, because my day was about to change direction in a major way. Everything about my life was about to go downhill.

Rapidly.

Chapter 24

The Best Foundation Starts with a Brush

Here's a tip I learned from a makeup artist: The best way to put on makeup foundation is with a brush, not a sponge or—worst of all—your fingers. And you should make sure to use a well-tapered, synthetic brush. Natural brushes absorb too much foundation and skin oil and can lead to an uneven result.

—From *The Little Book of Beauty Secrets* by Mimi Morgan

"Come with me to zee casbah tonight, Kate. I have a sultan's son I want you to meet. He has a magic flying carpet."

"Evelyn, the *last* thing I want to do right now is meet someone new. I haven't even officially broken up with Jonathan yet. I haven't talked to him since I caught him in bed with Gi. Besides, I just made a fresh batch of sour cream onion dip."

I was sprawled out on the couch in my living room, covered in sour cream potato chip crumbs, holding my cell phone to my ear. Elfie was perched in her favorite spot—atop my chest, purring, with her paws tucked underneath her.

Evelyn and I had just finished doing a sobby postmortem of all the recent developments of the week, including Jana's murder. Now she had pulled out a bad Greta Garbo accent in an effort to lure me out of the comfy cocoon of my apartment on a Saturday night.

Over the phone, I heard Evelyn sigh. "Okay, so maybe the sultan's son I have in mind has a vintage Camaro, not a carpet," she said. "But that doesn't mean you should sit around the house on a Saturday night moping. Or *eating*."

That little dig made me regret having confessed my plunge into the chip dip.

As I covered the phone to muffle the sound of my crunching down on another chip, Evelyn continued, "Seriously, Kate—the ZuZubees are playing at the Metrodale tonight. I know the lead guitarist in the band really well. He's dying to meet you."

"I'll bet."

"Well, maybe I haven't exactly *mentioned* you to him yet. But still, he'll be thrilled to meet you once we're there. So please come to the club tonight with Kyle and me."

"Kyle? Who's he? What happened to Liam?"

"Oh, Liam had major baggage," she said, dismissing the discarded Liam with a sniff. "He couldn't stop complaining about his ex-wife. He called her his *ex-hole*; can you believe that? How boorish. So I ended the evening early. I didn't even let him see my new boobs."

"Serves him right."

Although I appreciated my friend's offer of companionship, I dreaded the idea of becoming a third wheel in a new love formation between Evelyn and some guy. And no way did I want to be introduced to a lead guitarist who undoubtedly preferred his groupies googly-eyed and tramp stamped.

"Thanks, Evelyn," I said. "But I think I just want to isolate tonight."

"Watch out for that urge to be alone," she warned. "You could slide into a depression."

"I'm fine. Don't worry."

"No, you're not. Anyone can have a few down days, Kate, but you've been stuck in this rut for a while. I'm no doctor, but I think you're clinically depressed. I think you should go see someone."

"I'm not—"

"No, really. I've known you a long time, and I'm worried about you. You're eating your redlight foods again, you're not going to the gym with me, and you never want to go out anymore. Those are the signs."

When I started to protest that I didn't have

any signs, she cut me off. "Yes, you do. You're almost turning into a hermit," she said. "You used to love going out clubbing with me."

"We'll go clubbing in the spring, okay? I really just feel like hibernating tonight."

"Hibernating?" Evelyn's tone was skeptical. "That's only for bears. When you're with a guy, it's called 'cocooning.' But when you're by yourself, you have a tendency to put on back fat."

"I'll go to yoga with you next week, okay?"

After we said good-bye and clicked off, I detached Elfie from my chest and gently set her down on the floor. Then I heaved myself to my feet and made my way to the kitchen. A wave of fatigue washed over me, and I felt as if I could barely stay upright. Maybe it was sugar withdrawal. Or maybe Evelyn was right—maybe I *was* depressed. All I'd had to eat today were refined carbohydrates—the really evil ones that had nothing in them except major injections of high-fructose corn syrup; someone had once told me that that was what they gave to people in cults to get them to break down mentally. It was time to check out the kitchen for something green and healthy.

I was reaching into my refrigerator when Elfie froze. She scrambled for the bedroom. Before I could figure out what had startled her, I heard a light tapping at the door.

I opened the door and felt a cool rush of air. An angular, familiar silhouette was framed in the camphor-colored light of the shallow front landing.

It was Jonathan.

Chapter 25

Jonathan stood in the doorway cradling an enormous bouquet of burgundy roses in his arms.

"Hi, Kate," he said. "Sorry to come by unannounced. I tried to call. Is it okay if I come in?"

Jonathan's voice sounded weighted down. It was hard to register exactly *how* he sounded, because the sight of him had kicked up a sudden sandstorm of emotions inside me. A million tiny shards of feeling blew out of the desert, wiping out clear thought.

"Of course you can come in." I swiped the

back of my hand across my cheek to brush away any lingering specks of potato chips.

He still had those amazing back-lit blue eyes that I'd fallen for. The rest of his face looked worn and scruffy, as if he hadn't slept or shaved. Normally Jonathan was perfectly groomed and dressed.

I backed into the living room and dropped onto the vintage bergère chair that I'd bought at a yard sale a few months earlier. Gripping its upholstered arms, I sat there like a woman who was waiting for someone to throw the switch.

Jonathan laid the roses on the coffee table, then took a seat on the couch. The sweet fragrance of the flowers wafted through the room. As we faced each other across the coffee table in silence, I decided not to go for a vase.

Jonathan's unexpected arrival made me wish I could be teleported by some alien technology into a faraway galaxy—preferably a galaxy named Before. I yearned for that universe because it was the one that had existed before I learned that Jonathan had slept with Gi.

Elfie floated in from the bedroom with her tail rising above her like a plume. Approaching Jonathan cautiously, she took a probing sniff. Then her whiskers twitched, and she made a little purring sound of happiness.

"Hey there, beautiful kitty." Jonathan stroked

the cat, who proceeded to jump into his lap. After making a couple of turns, she settled into a contented ball.

Elfie's arrival seemed to put a tiny chip in the ice between us. Jonathan looked at me and said, "Did you get my phone messages? I left several of them."

"Four," I said. "No, I didn't get them. I mean, I did, but I didn't listen to them. I deleted them."

"Oh."

The Adam's apple bobbed up and down slowly in Jonathan's neck. "I wanted to tell you how sorry I was," he said. "That episode with Gi— that never should have happened."

"That *episode*? You're right, Jonathan. It never should have happened. But it did. Why did it?"

"It's a long, awful story. The bottom line is—I never wanted to hurt you, Kate."

"You've more than hurt me, Jonathan," I said. "You've destroyed everything we had together as a couple. I really thought we were special. To me, you were special."

"Please don't talk like that."

"But it's true."

Closing my eyes, I heard the heat rise on each syllable as I continued, "You've *killed* us, Jonathan. You're a homicide cop, right? You know what murder is, right? That's what you've done to us. Murder one."

"Kate."

I heard a commotion. When I opened my eyes, Elfie was scrambling to escape from the room again and Jonathan was bending over me; cupping my face with his hands; whispering urgently in my ear.

"Please. Please, love," he said, bending down with one knee on the floor. "I wish more than the world that I could erase what happened. I know it's impossible to ask you to forgive me. But please don't ever think I don't love you. Because I do. More than you can even know right now."

He lowered his head onto my lap and rested it there.

With his voice muffled against my stomach, he continued, "All I want to do is make it up to you. I want to make things right. Please, Kate. Let me make things right."

Gently, I rested my hand on top of his hair. The hair felt soft, but my wrist was locked tight. I felt an eerie sense of detachment from what was happening.

Something about Jonathan's head in my lap and his being down on one knee made it feel like we were acting out a tawdry scene from the life of Queen Elizabeth. Jonathan was playing the straying Sir Walter Raleigh, a supplicant waiting for the royal nod of forgiveness for the sin of bedding down a comely maiden he'd tripped across in a scullery. That made me the Virgin Queen, I guessed. My fingers went icy.

I couldn't manage to connect any emotion to what was happening between us. I especially couldn't connect to what was happening with Jonathan.

The man kneeling in front of me didn't seem at all like the man I knew. This man wasn't the emotionally reserved homicide cop I'd fallen in love with. *This* man was acting like someone who was veering on the edge of an emotional meltdown. What the hell had happened to him since he'd left the United States on his vacation? Had Gi cast some kind of bizarre sex spell over him? Clearly I was going to have to get to know my boyfriend all over again if we were going to put things back together. If I was *willing* to put things back together, that is.

Once before a boyfriend had cheated on me. At the time it hadn't seemed like a difficult situation. Enraging and humiliating, yes, but not difficult. When that guy had confessed his betrayal to me over lunch, I'd blessed him and his new tramp with an Irish curse and never spoken to him again. I never even looked back. But I hadn't been in love with him.

Jonathan was a completely different story. What was I going to do?

Jonathan says he loves me. Jonathan says he's

sorry. Jonathan is down on his knees. Jonathan is begging me to forgive him.

The phrases ran together in my head in an endless loop. It was a manic parrot song of love and remorse, sung in a British accent.

Forgive him. Was it ever going to be possible for me to do that?

It was much too soon to tell.

Chapter 26

V-necks for Large Busts

If you have a large chest, usually the most flattering neckline is a V-neck. Don't be afraid to show a little cleavage. Hold the line at one and a half inches, though—an excessive cleavage line is matronly. And besides, you don't want the girls to look like they're going to fall onto the table. That's just cheap.

—From *The Little Book of Beauty Secrets* by Mimi Morgan

An hour later Jonathan and I were lying on top of the duvet that covered my bed. Fully clothed and not touching, we were stretched out like two dolls that had been placed next to each other.

In halting sentences Jonathan began to reveal the story of how he'd met Gi. They'd met eight years earlier during a trip he'd made to China. She was working as a bar girl in Beijing. She'd escaped from North Korea, but she was being abused by the smugglers who'd brought her in. They were forcing her to work as a prostitute, Jonathan told me.

"For all practical purposes, Gi was working as a sex slave when I met her," Jonathan explained.

Staring up at the popcorn ceiling of my bedroom, he continued. "What she was doing back then wasn't by her choice. She was being threatened by the smugglers who got her over the border. I felt I had to get her out of there. I made arrangements to bring her home to England with me."

"What arrangements?"

"We got married. I paid to have her paperwork doctored. It's the only time in my life I've ever committed a crime."

He closed his eyes. "I was studying criminology back in the UK at the time," he said. "I could have gone to jail for what I did. I'm not proud of that."

"You must have loved her very much."

"Yes, but what I felt for Gi back then was more than love. And less in a strange way. I can only describe it as a burning thing . . . as an *obsession*. For a while I think I really lost my mind over her. I was capable of doing anything for her back then."

Each word that Jonathan was saying was dripping onto my brain like burning oil, causing incredible agony. But I was determined to keep listening. I had a ludicrous, sudden urge to grab a tape recorder to record our conversation because my brain was in too much shock to fully absorb everything he was saying. It was unbearable to hear more.

Gi had turned out to be dangerously unstable, Jonathan told me. "She was—is—extremely insecure about money," he said. "She kept incessantly looking for ways for us to become rich overnight. She thought we had to have pots of money, or else she'd wind up back on the streets, back in North Korea. That made no sense. I'm a *cop*.

"Gi couldn't stand the thought that I'd never earn big money. In the end she found some bloke she thought could give her all the material things she wanted. I came home early one afternoon and found them in bed together."

"What did you do?"

"I walked out and never saw her again."

"Until this week."

"Until eight months ago."

"You saw her eight *months* ago?"

"Briefly, when I went home for the Christmas holidays. Remember? You couldn't come because you had to work."

"Don't you dare try to blame this situation on my work, Jonathan. You slept with Gi eight *months* ago? And you haven't told me anything in all this time?"

"I didn't know what to say at the time, Kate."

Right. What could he have said? Our relationship would have been over eight months ago. Curling my hands into fists, I pressed them into my stomach. At some stronger time in the future I'd have to rewrite our emotional history as a couple. So many huge things had gone unsaid between us. How could I not have felt that something was desperately wrong on some level? For the past eight months, the only negative emotion I'd felt was insecurity about my body. Probably that insecurity had masked deeper worries running beneath the surface. A psychologist would have a field day with me.

After a painful silence, Jonathan resumed speaking. "Gi has stayed close to my mum all these years," he said. "Gi took care of Mum, and I guess she used her as a sort of refuge whenever she got in trouble. Last Christmas I told Gi to stay away while I was there, but one night she came over with some woolly socks and teas for Mum. I got drunk and—"

"And the rest I can figure out. And fuck you, by the way. Unless you care to describe how much you enjoyed your little Gi fling. Was she nice and tight, Jonathan? Is that what you've been missing all this time?"

"Please don't, Kate. I hate to hear you talk like that. That's not like you at all."

"Spare me the language lecture, Jonathan. And

don't tell me what I'm *like*. Whatever I'm like, it obviously isn't sufficient for you. You were in bed with Gi this week, right? When I called and she grabbed the phone?"

Jonathan's face was rigid. "Not in that . . . way. There was no intimacy between us this time. Not on this trip."

"Well, say hallelujah for *that*. So what exactly were you doing when Gi said you two were fucking like love bunnies?"

"We weren't having sex, Kate. That's just Gi's craziness."

"If you expect me to believe that, Jonathan, then you must think I'*m* crazy."

Jonathan shifted to one side and looked into my eyes. "I don't think you're crazy," he said. "I think you're sanest woman I've ever met. But I let you down. I know that I did."

His voice turned leaden and defeated as he continued. "I have to tell you everything now."

"You mean there's *more*?"

"Yes."

God.

"But first I want you to know," he said. "There's nothing left emotionally between Gi and me. Absolutely nothing."

"Absolutely nothing but a little vacation sex every few years?"

"Please, Kate. Can I just finish what I have to say?"

When I shrugged, he resumed, "I have no feelings for Gi anymore except for maybe pity. There's nothing left in my heart and hasn't been for a long time. But . . ."

Something bad was coming. Something that was even worse than being cheated on. Instinctively I rolled away from him.

Jonathan shielded his eyes with his hand. "Gi's eight months pregnant," he said. "She says she conceived during that one time we were together at the Christmas holiday.

"Gi says the baby is mine."

Chapter 27

A Personal Grooming Tool

I wish I'd known about facial-grooming tools long ago—it would have spared me a lot of episodes of embarrassing chin hair. Usually battery operated, the grooming tool is used to whisk away facial hairs. You can also use it to remove the hair in the ... ahem, delicate areas of your body.

Make sure you invest in a good-quality tool. The better-made facial groomers are a bit more expensive but well worth the price.

—From *The Little Book of Beauty Secrets* by Mimi Morgan

"She's pregnant? Gi is having your *baby*?"

Oh God oh God oh God. Oh, Jesus.

A blinding pain shot through my head. "Tell me everything else *right now*, Jonathan," I gasped. "Are you even *divorced*? On the phone Gi said she's still your wife."

"Not technically."

"Not divorced *technically*? You're a cop, for God's sake!"

"Not technically, because the original paperwork was doctored. I can't even get a legitimate divorce in England. Right now, legally I'm stuck with her. It's like I made a deal with the devil when I smuggled her in."

More like he'd *married* the devil. And now she was having the devil's child.

The second that thought entered my head, the ghost of my Catholic upbringing reared its disapproving head and glared at me. Quickly, I made the sign of the cross over my chest. Back in grade school, the nuns had taught me that it was a serious sin to condemn an unborn baby, even in one's thoughts. No matter how unstable Gi was or what Jonathan had done, their baby was God's precious being. Never a spawn of the devil.

I hadn't made the sign of the cross since I was thirteen years old. And I hadn't been to a priest to make a confession in nearly that long. Clearly I was overdue.

At the sight of my making the sign of the cross, Jonathan sat upright in the bed. He had a nervous look on his face.

And he had plenty of cause to be afraid. I was like an IED ready to go off. It was all I could do to keep my finger from releasing the trigger button.

"You better go home now, Jonathan," I said, heaving with the desire to claw at him.

"I don't want to go. I think we need to talk some more."

"I don't want to talk to you. Get out of my house right now, because I don't want to be charged with assaulting an officer."

He reached for my hand. "Don't be ridicu—"

"Get *out* of here!"

The hand he'd touched exploded. My fingers unfurled and slashed across his face.

Jonathan didn't try to defend himself or control me. A drop of his blood remained on my finger as I pulled it away, smearing the linen pillowcase.

I didn't pause to consider that I'd drawn blood; rage had taken the driver's seat. I pushed Jonathan out of my bed and drove him before me. In the living room Jonathan opened the front door, then held on to the knob for a few seconds while I screamed foul-sounding names at him. I don't even know what kinds of things I was screaming. I wasn't even Kate Gallagher anymore. I was a Greek Fury, only with a vocabulary of pithy Irish insults.

After an uncertain amount of time passed in this drama, the sound of a dog's barking jerked me into awareness of the world around us. In the house next door to mine, the older lady who heads our neighborhood watch group had emerged onto her lighted front porch. She was holding her Rottweiler by its collar.

"Dear, are you okay? Do you need the dog,

or shall I call the police?" she called to me in a worried-sounding voice.

"No, it's okay. He *is* the police," I replied. "I'm very sorry for the disturbance. Don't worry, ma'am. We're fine."

Except that we weren't. We never would be again.

The neighbor's intervention had lanced my boil's rage, releasing its pressure. I turned my head away from Jonathan.

"Go on now, Jonathan," I said, closing my eyes. "Just go away."

When I opened them again, he was gone.

I backed up against the couch and dropped onto it. I remained there for a very long time, dimly aware of the changes of light and cooling air coming through my front door, which was still open a few inches. At some point I must have closed it.

I snapped out of my trance when the alarm clock buzzer in the bedroom went off. It was five a.m.

My gaze landed on the dark red roses that Jonathan had brought with him earlier. I picked them up off the table and cradled them against me for a long moment, inhaling their delicate fragrance. I walked with them outside.

The morning air felt cool and moist against my skin as I headed down the sidewalk in front of my house. Destination: a Dumpster located in front of a house that was being built down the street.

In front of the Dumpster I hesitated a moment, cradling the damp-stemmed roses against me. Their fragrance mixed in my nostrils with the smells of concrete and sawdust from the construction bin. Then I heaved the bouquet into the trash. The roses broke apart in the air, scattering petals into the bin and the sidewalk below.

I walked away.

Chapter 28

It was Sunday morning at eleven a.m., the time of day when many people in Durham were dressed up in their Sunday clothes, heading to their places of worship to bow their heads in prayer.

Inside Durham County Jail on East Main Street, a much less reverential scene was taking place. Antoine Hurley, accused murderer of Jana Miller, was sitting across from me in the inmates' visitors room on the opposite side of a plastic partition. He was dressed in the orange scrubs of a county inmate, and his head was bowed. But not in prayer. Antoine was just eighteen years old, and he didn't look like a murderer. He looked as scared as hell.

Antoine's lawyer, Miles Goldberg, had arranged for me to bring a videographer to shoot some video of his client. We weren't allowed to talk through the plastic partition—the lawyer would do all the talking later.

To hear Luke or any other cop describe Antoine, the boy was nothing but a gangbanger who'd killed Jana for easy money. Luke had called Antoine a "scumbag." But that description didn't jibe with what I was seeing through the divider between us. Antoine had the soft, studious features of a mathlete, right down to the rimless glasses. We sat opposite each other without speaking, which felt supremely weird. In fact it felt almost invasive, like Antoine had been trucked out to be videotaped like some kind of zoological specimen.

Antoine sat motionless for several moments, staring down at the graffiti-scarred desk in front of him. Then abruptly, he shifted to the side and reached into his pocket for something.

I felt a surge of alarm, even though there was a plastic partition between us. Then I realized that the object that Antoine was pulling from his pocket was a piece of paper, not a weapon.

Staring at me with large, liquid brown eyes that were rimmed with black lashes, Antoine held the paper up to the plastic. He flattened it out so that I could read the writing.

In careful, square-edged lettering, the paper said:

> *When you see my mama, please tell her that I love her.*
> *And please tell her that I'm sorry.*

An hour later Frank and I were riding in the broadcast truck, on our way to interview Antoine's mother. They lived in the Centerville projects in east Durham. If you want to get an idea of what the projects are like, take any bad section of town you've ever seen, and then quadruple it. Then add streets patrolled by sociopaths carrying automatic weapons. That gives you the flavor of Centerville. It's the worst of the urban worst. I knew from Jonathan that the cops donned full-body Kevlar armor and brought plenty of backup whenever they responded to an incident in the projects. They always had to be prepared to deal with the M Street Crew gang, which controlled the streets. Allegedly, Antoine was a gunman for that gang.

I had to find out whether that was true.

Chapter 29

"Vanish" Your Lines
with a Klingon Cloaking Device

*We all fret about "marionette lines," the ones that run
from the nose to the lips, and from the edges of the
lips to the chin. To minimize them, first dot a highlight-
ing concealer along the lines. Then use your synthetic
foundation brush to blend in the concealer. It'll do
wonders for "lifting" those downward-drooping marionette lines.*

—From *The Little Book of Beauty Secrets* by Mimi Morgan

"I know everyone thinks my Antoine is a cold-
blooded murderer. But they don't know my son.
Only *I* know him. My Antoine would never, ever
kill anyone. He's a good boy."

Violet Hurley stared at me across the wooden
table. We were sitting in her well-appointed and
immaculately clean kitchen. A picture of Christ,
his eyes cast upward and hands clasped in prayer,
hung on the wall over the sink. Several tall vo-
tive candles were lined up on the window ledge.
All were lit.

Next to Violet was a trim man who sat on the edge of the kitchen chair at an angle. He radiated intensity. It was Antoine's lawyer, Miles Goldberg. He was a well-known criminal defense attorney in the tristate area.

Just for the record, I did *not* want to do this story. Lainey had handled all the stories so far about Jana's carjacking and Antoine's arrest. In fact, she'd done little more than regurgitate what officials had told her on the record. But Beatty had insisted that I do this one, for some reason. When I objected, orders came down from the GM for me to do the piece. God knows why they had a bug up their ass. Maybe they thought Lainey's police stories were too soft.

But because this story involved my friend's murder, I was uncomfortable in the extreme. I'd have to summon up all my objectivity to remain professional.

Frank, who had his camera on a tripod in the corner of the room, was adjusting the lens focus. He gave me a nod to indicate that we were ready to roll tape.

I looked at Violet. "Mrs. Hurley, why do you think the police arrested Antoine if he's innocent?"

"I'll answer that question," Goldberg the lawyer interjected smoothly. "We believe that Antoine is being blamed for a crime that was

actually committed by someone else. By someone in the M Street Crew gang."

Rolling up a ball of tissue in her hand, Violet
said, "I told Antoine, 'Stay clear of those M Crew
boys; you'll wind up dead. They're killers.' I told
him and told him. Now look at what's happened. That poor woman died, her child got
hurt, and they're blaming my son. *My son.* He's
an honor student at his high school. He gets all
As. Did the police tell you about that?"

"No, they didn't," I said.

"They never do. Not when they've already decided who they want to hang for the crime."

I looked at Goldberg. "What about the witness
ID?"

Goldberg cast a sideways glance at Violet.
"Are you okay to hear these details, Violet?"

Violet scrubbed the tears off her cheeks with
the tissue. "Please go ahead, Mr. Goldberg. I
want to hear everything about my son's case.
The good *and* the bad," she said with a quiet
dignity.

"Antoine hijacked the Miller's car; that's true,"
Goldberg began, looking at me. "But he was
forced to do it. And despite what the police are
saying, Antoine didn't have a gun. Gang members were threatening to kill him and his family.
That's the way that gang operates. Violet filed

several complaints about the fact that the M Street Crew had been threatening her and her son. But the police did nothing."

"That's right, Mr. Goldberg," Violet said, rocking back and forth in her chair. "If you live in the projects, you're invisible to the police. Only when somebody gets killed do they bother to show up. Especially when someone from *outside* this area gets killed. I hope you'll do a story on that someday, Miss Gallagher."

"It sounds like I should," I said.

Goldberg leaned toward me. "The bottom line is that my client Antoine had nothing to do with killing Mrs. Miller," he said, keeping his eyes fastened on mine. "They forced him to get in that car."

"Forced?"

"Yes. Someone with a gun forced Antoine into that car, and that was the person who later shot Mrs. Miller."

"Who?"

"It was Mad Dog!" Violet blurted out the name in a scream.

Covering her eyes with her hands, she continued, "Mad Dog told Antoine they needed the car to go to a party, and then they were going to dump it. Antoine was afraid not to do what Mad Dog said. Everyone is. Mad Dog will kill you as soon as look at you. It's terrible out there for young men these days, Miss Gallagher."

Goldberg glanced at Violet. "Mad Dog's real name is Akito Carver. He's a major narco dealer with ties to Miami cartels."

Removing a picture from another folder, he pushed it toward me. "This is Akito Carver. Also known as Mad Dog."

The photo showed a young African-American male with shoulder-length dreadlocks.

At the sight of the photo, Violet visibly recoiled "Mad Dog's a monster," she said. "My son is getting punished for what *he* did."

I felt sorry for Violet, but so far I wasn't convinced by what the lawyer was saying about Mad Dog being Jana's shooter.

"The eyewitness only saw Antoine during the hijacking, from what I've heard," I said, thinking of Shaina.

"But she didn't see Antoine *shoot* Mrs. Miller," Goldberg said. "She couldn't have. The shooting happened a couple of minutes later. And Mad Dog was the shooter. He and a couple of his friends were parked around the corner in another vehicle. And he had the gun. He *always* has a gun."

"That's a good story. But where's the evidence to support what you're saying?"

Goldberg handed me a folder. "An indepen-

dent forensics lab has concluded that the angle of
the bullets that killed Jana Miller couldn't have
been fired from inside the car where Antoine
was," he said. "They came from outside the car."

"From the *outside* of the car?"

"Yes. But you won't hear about any of this
from the prosecution's side—they'll be testi*lying*
all the way through this case," he said, using a
defense attorney's portmanteau for police officers'
alleged habit of lying on the stand.

I couldn't believe the prosecution would let
anyone lie on the witness stand, but I was
stunned by the report I had in my hand. If it
was correct, it was clear evidence that the bullets
that killed Jana came from outside her vehicle.
How, then, could the police accuse Antoine of
killing her?

"Shaina *did* say she never saw a gun in Antoine's hand," I said. "And she lost sight of the
car before she heard the shots."

"Exactly. And those shots were fired by Mad
Dog. He was lying in wait for the car."

I flipped through the rest of the report. It
would take some time to go through all the technical details, but the summary indicated that
what the lawyer was saying was true—Antoine
couldn't have fired the shots that killed Jana.

When I looked up from reading, Violet and the
lawyer were quietly conferring. I took in our sur-

roundings. The Hurley home was pleasant and well kept, but it seemed highly unlikely that she would be able to afford the services of an attorney such as Miles Goldberg, whose rates started at more than four hundred dollars an hour.

"How'd you happen to take on Antoine's case, Mr. Goldberg?" I asked the lawyer.

Goldberg shot me an evaluating look. "Are you asking whether it's pro bono?"

Violet straightened up in her chair. "The Hurley family doesn't take charity from anyone, Miss Gallagher," she said. "I'm using Antoine's college savings to pay for his defense. We'll go into debt—we'll go broke if we have to—but my boy will have the best defense money can buy."

"I'm sorry if I seemed to imply anything else," I said, chagrined. So much for my theory that Gavin was paying for Antoine's defense.

By the time we left Violet Hurley's apartment, the atmosphere in the projects' central court had a festive feel to it—everyone had heard that the TV news was doing a story about Antoine. Word was beginning to spread that it might be sympathetic to his case.

I planned to do everything possible to make the story fair to both sides. Based on my interview with Antoine's mother and the attorney, there was an entirely new question to be considered.

Luke had been so positive that Antoine had been the one who pulled the trigger on the gun that killed Jana. Could he have been wrong?

Was Antoine innocent?

Chapter 30

My story about Antoine aired on the late news Sunday night. Early Monday morning, I walked into a firestorm of criticism. A string of irate messages was waiting for me when I arrived at the newsroom at eight a.m. The worst of them was from Luke Petronella of Durham Homicide.

"What the hell got into you last night, running that tabloid trash about Antoine Hurley?" the detective's message began. "Don't you know that every gangbanger in the world claims that he was 'coerced' into going along with the crime? Shit. It was your friend he killed, Kate. Are you out of your *mind*?"

As I cringed back in my desk chair, Luke continued his rampage. "So listen up—from now on, I'm not giving you shit about my investigation," he said. "You want a comment about a story, you call Public Relations. And you can go fuck yourself while you're at it. You were *way* out of line to let some shiny-suit lawyer raise questions in public about my case. Fucking lawyers. You're shit on my shoe, Gallagher. Total shit!"

I'd never been raked over the coals like that by someone I respected like Luke. And there was much more like that to come. The nicer callers implied that I was shilling for Antoine's defense. The nastiest one said my mother should have aborted me in the womb. Most of the callers simply implied that I'd earned my journalism degree from an online school for hacks.

Good grief. They *hated* me. Maybe Evelyn had had a point when she said I was clinically depressed. I'd never felt so low, so barely alive. It felt as if my body's vital signs were registering in the zombie zone.

I was hunched over the phone in my cubicle, sipping coffee and scribbling notes about each call, when Beatty appeared at the opening to my cubicle.

"Hey—you need to listen to something on the police scanner," he said, nodding toward the assignment desk.

I slunk along in my boss's wake, mentally girding for the worst.

A bunch of news reporters were leaning around the assignment desk, monitoring the police scanner. The assembled crowd included Dutch Kramer, the sportscaster.

"Hey, Kate," Dutch said, tossing me a loopy-looking grin. "You're the hot topic this morning on the squawk box."

"Oh, yeah, Dutch? How's that?"

"They're saying you should get a big hairy one up the ass for that story you did last night about Antoine Hurley."

"Thanks for sharing that."

I rested my knuckles on the desktop and listened as disembodied cops' voices squawked over the scanner.

"That hit piece she did last night was a complete piece of crap," one cop said. "They oughta fire that Gallagher woman's fat ass."

"The whole thing's bullshit, man," another responded. "Whose side is that reporter on, anyway? The f'n shooter's?"

The cops in the squad cars had to be aware that we monitored their exchanges over our scanner, as did every other media outlet in town. They undoubtedly meant to be overheard. I was being skewered in a most public, graphic way.

It was more than a bit disconcerting, especially since the case involved my friend's murder.

Just great. I hadn't wanted to do that story in the first place, and now I was being blamed.

I stood by my story—it was a solid piece—but still, the anonymous criticism by the cops raised the hair on the back of my neck: *Whose side is that reporter on, anyway? The f'n shooter's?*

My colleagues were chattering and bouncing oddly energized looks off me. There's nothing that gets the adrenaline going for journalists like provoking the wrath of police officialdom. But you better not get caught making a mistake in your reporting. That would be a job killer.

"Hey, I love being tarred and feathered in public," I said, trying to make light of the situation.

I waited with bated breath for Beatty to render his verdict. You never knew which way the news-directorial wind would blow.

"Way to go at 'em in that piece last night, Gallagher," Beatty said finally. "You'll notice that they aren't challenging your *facts*. If they were, the chief of police would have been crawling up my ass already by now this morning. They're just pissed off we ran something for once that didn't parrot their side of this story."

The news parrot in question—Lainey—stood a few feet away. She was staring intently at the cable TV monitors on the wall. But I could tell by her defensive body posture that her ears and reporter's ego were burning. Too bad.

Beatty was pleased with my story about Antoine Hurley. In maritime terms, a nod from the Big Boss was the equivalent of starting the day off with a fair wind and a following sea.

"Hey, Kate!" Frank called out. He was standing near my desk. "Phone!"

I dashed to grab the phone, even though it was probably just another caller who couldn't wait to describe how my reporting had stunk up the airwaves.

"Hi, Kate. It's Belmont Miller. Jana's brother."

It took me a moment to connect the name with the identity.

Jana's brother, Belmont. When we'd last spoken, Belmont had been on his way to the Bahamas, taking Shaina with him so she could recover from her carjacking ordeal and the death of her mother.

"Hi, Belmont—are you all still in the Bahamas?" I asked him. "How is Shaina doing? How's her recovery coming?"

"Shaina's doing fine. But I'm calling about something else. Did you hear about what we found out about Jana's autopsy?" Belmont's voice rose with emotion. "Goddammit, they're not going to get away with this. Someone in the police department is going to pay!"

My mind flailed about, trying to figure out what the heck he was talking about.

"Wait a second—slow down, Belmont," I said. "What are you saying about Jana's autopsy? What's happened, exactly?"

"We just heard back from the firm we hired to do a second, private autopsy on her," Belmont said. "They told us that Jana's body was mutilated."

"Mutilated? I don't understand. The police already did a standard autopsy. Is that what you're talking about?"

"Something was done to her body *after* the police autopsy but before we got the body, according to my people. While she was still in the custody of the medical examiner's office, someone surgically removed some tissue from her body.

"They stole her heart valve. It's missing from her body."

Chapter 31

"What?" I asked, not sure exactly what I'd heard. "Somebody removed Jana's *heart valve*? Wait a minute—are you sure that wasn't part of the medical examiner's autopsy procedure? Sometimes they remove body organs, don't they?"

"Of course they do," Belmont replied in an impatient tone. "But this is *not* standard procedure. My lawyer told me heart valves can fetch up to ten grand on the black market, even from . . . even from cadavers. I guess when they use cadaver valves in research, med schools don't ask too many questions."

"So—"

"So somebody in the medical examiner's office thought they could make a quick killing by taking the heart valve from my sister's body."

"Have you told the homicide detectives about this yet?"

"I'm not going to waste my time talking to those clowns," he replied. "If they have to learn this from me, they're incompetent. I don't want any of them anywhere near her."

"I understand," I said, reaching for a notepad and a pen on my desk. "Is it okay if I jot down some notes about this conversation, Belmont? I might run a story about what's happened."

"Be my guest," he replied. "You can write that I'm suing the city of Durham for all that Podunk city's worth, just to show them they need to learn how to do their jobs better. How do I even know the police have arrested the right suspect when they screw up Jana's autopsy like this? Who stole her heart valve? I mean, it's nothing compared to her murder, but they're a bunch of damned incompetents, in my opinion. You always get the D team in the government."

"What's happening these days with Jana's widower, by the way?"

"Widower? Hah! That's a kind term," Belmont

said. "I've tied up Gavin's insurance settlement in court. I don't think that blondie girlfriend of his is going to wait around long enough for him to become a rich man."

After getting the name and number of Belmont Miller's lawyer, I decided to put in a call to Luke. But for that I'd need to screw up some major courage.

"I'm not talking to you," Luke said when he picked up the phone.

"I can hear that."

"Just so we're clear."

"We are," I said. "I was just wondering if you heard about Jana's heart valve being removed during the autopsy. Supposedly by someone in the medical examiner's lab."

A pause. Followed by "You'll have to ask them."

"You're in charge of the investigation, Luke. What do *you* say?"

"On the record? No comment."

"And off the record?"

"Make a Xerox and tack it up on your cube."

"C'mon. This could screw up your case against Antoine Hurley real bad, couldn't it? The defense could have a field day with the fact that Jana's heart valve was stolen while the county had custody of her body. It won't exactly take a Dream Team to make that argument."

"Since when did you become the spokesman for the defense of Antoine Hurley?"

"For the *defense*? Luke, Jana's family told me about her missing heart valve. Her brother, Belmont Miller, is the only spokesman I know about today. But for Jana, not for Antoine Hurley."

When Luke stayed silent, I went for blood. "And while we're discussing Jana, Luke, what's your reaction to the new independent lab evidence about the bullet that killed her?" I asked. "That the bullet came from outside the car. And if that turns out to be true, then Antoine couldn't have been the shooter the way you've been saying."

"Kate." Luke's voice was venomous. "I said, 'No comment.' What word did you not understand? No comment. No how, no way."

I didn't have a chance to come back after that, because Luke hung up.

That went pretty well, I thought, slumping back in my chair. Luke was saying that by showing Antoine's side of the story, I was trampling on the prosecution's side of the case.

When it came to identifying Jana's murderer, I only hoped I wasn't in danger of trampling on the truth.

Chapter 32

Banish the Clumps

Don't forget to use a lash comb after you apply your mascara. There's nothing tackier than clumpy, caked mascara.

—From *The Little Book of Beauty Secrets* by Mimi Morgan

As if I didn't have enough on my plate, Beatty chose that exact moment to bug me about my weight-loss series.

"How are your fat stories coming along?" He'd rematerialized at my cubicle.

"Fine," I lied. In fact, Frank and I had finished taping only the first segment of the weight-loss series, the Skinny Wrap story. We had four parts left to do.

"Good, because I want to move your series up on the schedule," he said. "We need to run the first two installments next week."

Next *week*? Yikes. I was supposed to have three more weeks to work on it.

"Okay, but I've got a lot of breaking stuff I'm

following right now," I said. "I just got an update about the Jana Miller carjacking."

Beatty waved off my objection. "Give your carjacking updates to someone else if you don't have time to handle everything," he said. "I need to get your series on the air ASAP. It's going to run instead of Lainey's series on homeless dumping."

At the mention of Lainey, my ears pricked up like a terrier puppy's.

"Why the switch?" I asked him. "What's wrong with her series?"

"It needs more reporting. Meanwhile, Marketing is screaming bloody murder down my back because we need something else pronto to promote for next week. We got squat right now."

Needs more reporting. That meant that Lainey had screwed the pooch on her stories, newswise. There was no time for me to do a victory dance, however, because I was woefully behind in completing my own series. Plus I was anxious to check into the report I'd heard from Jana's brother about how her body had been mishandled. That was a major scandal brewing in the medical examiner's office.

I gave Beatty a wild, hopeful look. "Maybe I could finish Lainey's homeless series for her. I could turn that one around really fast," I suggested. "I've already got solid sources for it."

Give me anything, God, but having to work on more fat rip-off stories. I sent up a little prayer.

Beatty lowered his aviators on his nose to peer at me. "Does that mean *your* series is ready to go right this second? Fine. Where's the disk?"

"I'm tweaking it."

"You're tweaking it. And I'm the wizard of friggin' Oz."

Beatty started to turn away. Then he snapped back around, his favorite method for catching reporters off guard. The Beatty Brows were working in hypermotion. If the rest of us were lucky, one of these days his eyebrows would sprout wings and fly away with his face.

"Are you *positive* you'll be ready with your first two installments by next week, Gallagher?" he demanded to know. "Because I need to review both of them by this Thursday. That's three days from now. That's a drop-dead date, by the way."

"You'll have both stories in your hands by this Thursday, Beatty. Don't worry—it's under control."

Yup. My fat-scam series was under control. Like everything else in my life these days, the series was about as under control as a plane that was nosing over into a death spiral.

Chapter 33

Make your Eyes Pop

For a daring, eye-popping look, add a few false lashes to the edges of your lash line. But here's the secret—cut the false lashes so that they're slightly shorter than your real ones. That way they'll add fullness and drama without going over the top into Liza Minnelli Land.

—From *The Little Book of Beauty Secrets* by Mimi Morgan

I had an interview scheduled for Tuesday morning with Evelyn's plastic surgeon, the much-ballyhooed Dr. Medina. I was going to test the "thermal-laser thingee" that Evelyn and the Newbodies group had been raving about. The procedure was actually called thermal laser-lite, and it was supposed to melt away your fat and shrink your skin. My job was to tell viewers whether it in fact worked.

When I'd called to arrange the interview with Medina, I didn't tell his scheduling assistant that there was a chance that the procedure might wind up on my list of fat scams. I actually hoped the wand worked, because I was going to be the guinea pig for a free round of laser lifting. Normally each treatment cost nearly a thousand dollars.

Off the record, I was hoping that I might even get Dr. Medina to talk a little bit about Jana, who'd been one of his patients. Jana had come straight from Dr. Medina's office to our lunch on the day before she was killed. I was even hoping that I might get some insight from Dr. Medina about the latest twist in her case, the alleged theft of her internal organs. As a medical doctor who dealt with the human body's largest organ— skin—Dr. Medina might have some background information that I could use.

Dr. Medina's plastic surgery office was several tax brackets more luxe than any doctor's office I'd ever seen before. The waiting room was centered by an enormous glass sculpture. Lit from within, the sculpture was formed in the shape of layered crystals and looked like something that might have been found in Superman's secret cave.

As Frank and I hauled our loads of equipment into the waiting room, a woman behind the long white counter gave me a welcoming smile.

"Kate Gallagher?"

When I nodded, she clapped her hands together. "Ooh, I'll be so excited to tell my daughter I got to meet you," she said in an excited-sounding tone. "Nadia is fourteen years old; she watches you on the news all the time. And so do I, by the way. I'm Michelle, Dr. Medina's assistant."

I felt completely disarmed. For some reason I'd been expecting Dr. Medina's assistant to be incredibly young, or else a study in filler-and-lasered perfection. Michelle appeared to be about fifty years old, and she seemed refreshingly un-lifted.

My first stop was the photo room, where I stepped up on a stool, and another assistant, this one a very young and insecure-looking woman named June, struggled to take my "before" picture.

After she reshot the series of front, side, rear, and other-side photos, June started sweating.

"Sorry, this is a brand-new camera," she kept saying.

It's hard to figure out what to do while you're being photographed for a "before" picture. Should you smile? Look depressed? Anything seems weird.

While I decided on an expression that I hoped looked appropriately natural, Miss June Bug of the Fumble Fingers kept fiddling around and apologizing for the malfunctioning camera.

After June's fourth retake, Frank rolled his eyes in exasperation behind her back.

"I'm going out to the truck for a spare battery," he said.

While Frank was gone, June finally got the shots she wanted. Then she gave me a dressing gown and ushered me into a small examination room.

"Dr. Medina will be in to see you in a moment," she said, and then withdrew, closing the door gently behind her.

I sat there reading women's magazines. Eventually, I heard a gentle tapping on the door.

"Come on in," I called out.

I found myself staring into a pair of warm, soulful brown eyes. George Clooney eyes. And they seemed to be smiling deep into my core.

Oh my God. Why didn't Evelyn tell me about those incredible *eyes*?

"Hello, Kate," the incredible man-creature who went with the eyes greeted me. "I'm Xavier Medina. So great to meet you."

"H-hi, Dr. Medina."

"Oh, please just call me Xavier. No ceremony here."

"Okay," I said, suddenly feeling shy. "Thanks so much for letting me and my crew do a story about your laser technique today."

When had I gotten so stiff and formal? That wasn't my usual style when doing a story.

"It's totally my pleasure—I've seen you on the television news, of course. Although I don't think of you as doing feature stories about skin treatments. Aren't you normally more of an investigative reporter? Big-time crime stuff?"

He gave me a knowing smile, as if we were both in on a clever joke. Dr. Medina—*Xavier*—exuded an air of confidence and competence. It was as if he already knew everything there was to know about my fat-scam series. And about me as well.

"Well, this *is* an investigative series of sorts, actually," I admitted. "I'm profiling what does and doesn't work in the area of fat loss."

"I'm glad to hear it. Based on what I've seen of your reporting, I know you'll be completely objective in your work. I want you to tell your audience exactly how you feel about the results of your thermal laser treatment—both the good *and* the bad," Xavier said smoothly.

He pulled up a stool. Then he donned a pair of goggles. Using a metal arm that extended with a lighted mirror on the end of it, he examined my face.

"I know we're treating your stomach, but I just have to say that your skin is amazing," he said. "Have you had IPL treatments or laser facials before?"

"No. What's amazing?"

"Your pores are unusually small. And you have very smooth, even coloration."

"Is that a bad thing?"

"It's a very *good* thing." Medina leaned back on his stool and laughed. "Women—and men, too—come in here and pay thousands of dollars to get what you've got."

"Really?"

"Yes. The small pores give your complexion a creamy, luminous surface. And you have almost no sun damage. It's very unusual, even in someone as young as you. You must not ever have been a sun worshipper."

"Really?"

I'd obviously just turned into a parrot whose only word was *Really? Really?* Which really must have made me sound like an idiot.

"Yes," he said. "Marilyn Monroe had your kind of skin, plus a fine layer of downy hair that caught the light just so. The effect was incredibly luminous—that's why the camera loved her so much. But the best example is a portrait I saw on a recent trip to Florence—have you ever seen the portrait of the Venus of Urbino, by chance? By Titian."

"I saw that portrait once on a trip after college," I said. "And I think I recall studying it in school."

Titian had painted the Venus of Urbino full length and buck-ass naked, with a fuck-me-now look in her eye. The painting had touched off a firestorm of court gossip during the Italian Renaissance, the same way the Paris Hilton tapes would hundreds of years later. Trust me to remember all the tabloid gossip from Art History 101.

Medina smiled as if he'd intercepted the raunchy little jog my thoughts had just taken. "Oops, sorry," he said. "I didn't mean to sound fresh. I just meant that your facial skin is like that Venus's. And actually so is the color of your hair."

His smile seemed to engulf his eyes as he continued, "I should add that I haven't seen a blush like yours in quite a while, either."

I could feel myself beginning to relax. Medina's compliments and gently probing questions made me feel truly *looked* at, for the first time in a long, long while. It was a flattering feeling. Intoxicating even. I was tempted to bask in that feeling and forget all about my story assignment.

While Medina excused himself to speak with June the photographer, who had knocked on the door to announce that she was struggling yet again with her camera, it occurred to me that I hadn't mentioned Jana to anyone at the office. Jana had been a patient of Dr. Medina's, plus

she'd seen him the day before she was killed. I
was dying to ask him about their last appointment. I knew he probably wouldn't violate doctor-
patient confidentiality by saying anything about
it. Still, it wouldn't hurt to ask. Maybe I'd learn
something new.

Medina was an interesting guy. And he *certainly* was attractive. Was it possible that he was
this friendly and charming with all his patients?
Maybe he was putting on a charm offensive for
me so that I'd do a positive news story about him.
That was always a possibility.

If he acted this way with everyone, I'd be surprised if the women of the Newbodies weren't
sending their underwear to him by Priority Mail.
I noticed he wasn't wearing a wedding ring.

Or *maybe* . . . maybe he was being this charming because he liked me. That thought squirted a
jet of heat into my cheeks. Then the heat spread
to a new location, this one completely inappropriate, given the clinical circumstances.

I'd just broken out with a severe case of Hot
Pants Fever for Dr. Xavier Medina.

Chapter 34

How to Wear Your Coats

Here's the trick to putting on mascara: Coat the top of your lashes with mascara first, with a downward stroke. Then coat the bottom of your lashes with an upward stroke.

—From *The Little Book of Beauty Secrets* by Mimi Morgan

"You're such a sucker for men's eyes, Kate," Evelyn said. "But really, you should have checked out his ass, too. Dr. Medina's butt is the absolute *most* awesome thing about him."

"If he hadn't been wearing a long white coat, believe me, I would have."

Actually I didn't care all that much about men's butts. I've never understood why women talk about them so much. To me, sexual attraction is all about a look in the eyes. Give me the right look in the eyes, and I'll follow you to the ends of the Milky Way.

Evelyn and I were having a late dinner at Christina's, a hole-in-the wall restaurant near my house in Trinity Heights. I loved the restaurant's aroma of hot garlic bread and fresh-made pasta. I even adored its unabashedly tacky décor, including the arbor of plastic grapes that hung in bunches from the ceiling.

"Okay, so here are some vital statistics about Dr. Medina that you should know," Evelyn said, spearing a frilly-edged leaf of escarole with her fork. "He's single, he's straight, and all the women in the Newbodies are totally gaga over him. But the word around the group is that he never dates patients. *Believe* me, I've tried. He just humors me."

"Technically speaking, Evelyn, I'm not Medina's patient. I'm a reporter doing a feature about him. That puts me on a slightly different footing."

"My, aren't you the little player?" Evelyn said with a roguish grin.

"No, not at all. This is a totally new feeling for me. I got the sense that Dr. Medina thinks I'm actually beautiful in a . . . in an *ideal* way. He actually compared me to the *Venus of Urbino*."

"To the *what*?"

"Titian's portrait of Venus. It's called the *Venus of Urbino*. He said I look like the painting. Did he ever say stuff like that to you?"

"You mean like Venus and Mars? Just kidding," Evelyn said. "No, he never said I look like a painting," Evelyn said. "The only thing he said before he did my boob job was that my left breast is a little bigger than the right one. He fixed that, though."

"I've never had a guy tell me that I look like an ideal beauty before. And he's an objective expert on the subject of looks, right? So he should know."

"Right. But sex isn't about being objective."

"I'm not talking about sex. I'm talking about surfaces—pure, unadulterated looks. Why did Medina, a plastic surgeon, compare me to a goddess of beauty? I have to believe he means it."

Evelyn waggled her fork at me. "Kate, you simply have to stop being surprised when men tell you you're gorgeous," she said. "I've been telling you that for years. So have lots of people. You just never believe us. The whole thing's getting to be a little disingenuous. Frankly, I'm annoyed by it."

"Sorry, but can you blame me?" I said. "Jonathan left my ego completely shredded. I'm a burned-out shell—I'm a walking straw woman, and he tossed a match on top of me. When I was in Medina's office and he said what he did to me . . . I don't know. It felt like he was rubbing a soothing balm into my *soul*. It was like he actually thought I was hot. Do you know what I mean?"

"I do know," Evelyn said. "We all need to feel sexy to our guys. It's a prerequisite. If it weren't for that, we'd probably be happier being with a gay guy. They usually make better friends."

"I used to tell myself that it was okay that my relationship with Jonathan was so reserved, because I knew underneath that he loved me. And anyway, I was the one who wouldn't let him in the shower when he asked to come in. I have to take responsibility for that."

I felt my chest heave up and down. A sob was trying to punch its way through my wall of self-control.

Evelyn reached for my hand. "Oh, sweetie," she said. "You've been through such a hard time. On the plus side, your depression must be lifting if you're obsessing about Dr. Medina. Just keep in mind that you're a woman on the rebound. I don't want you to set yourself up for more hurt."

"I'm not going after Medina," I said. "The whole idea is ridiculous. Besides, it would be completely cliché to fall for one's doctor right after a major breakup."

I hadn't fallen for Medina—not yet, anyway. For one thing, it was much too soon in the wake of the total demo-ing of my heart and soul by Jonathan and Gi.

But something about my encounter with the plastic surgeon the previous day had left an impression on my spirit—not to mention on my libido. Medina was definitely a hottie.

Evelyn giggled. "So what was your final verdict on the thermal-laser wand?" she asked. "Did it melt anything? You waist looks a little thinner, I think. Let me see."

I glanced around us. The only diners nearby were an older couple. They appeared to be completely absorbed by a plate of artisanal-looking bread and cheese.

"The jury's still out on the thermal-laser wand," I said. "Right now my stomach's still kind of swollen."

I lifted my blouse to demo my raw, still-healing midriff. It looked like I'd been hugged by a giant boa constrictor.

"Wow." Evelyn peered at my skin. "He did that with a *wand*? That's more bruising than I got with my implants."

"Aw, jeez. Really?"

The wand had actually been surprisingly painful. Even with the softening effect of a local anesthetic, it had felt like getting zapped by a cattle prod. The first time I'd felt the touch of the wand,

I jumped and let out a yelp. Frank had gotten that on tape, of course. It was certain to be the highlight of the marketing promo.

Talk about reporter involvement. If a shot of me squealing like a stuck pig and flopping around on top of a skin doctor's table didn't satisfy Beatty, nothing ever would.

Chapter 35

Sunscreen—the Best Skin Cream Around

There's only one skin cream in the world you need to use, and that's sunscreen. Make sure you wear it every day; put it on before you leave the house. Don't forget to put it on your hands, neck, and exposed chest areas—they get as much sun as your face!

—From *The Little Book of Beauty Secrets* by Mimi Morgan

Two hours, two orders of tiramisu, and a shared bottle of Chianti later, Evelyn and I were rehashing the latest developments in Jana's murder.

It was nearly nine thirty. My news story about Belmont Miller's allegations—that his sister's body organs had been stolen—was scheduled to air that night on the eleven o'clock news. I'd spent the entire day fleshing out the story (if you'll pardon the expression) with records from the firm that Belmont had hired to do the private autopsy on Jana, showing that her heart valve had been removed. I didn't use the video of her body that the firm had attached to an e-mail. Even if we blacked out her face, the video was far too gruesome. I wouldn't have used it even if Jana had been a total stranger.

My report had ended with my stand-up, in which I relayed a snippy "no comment" I'd gotten from the medical examiner's office in response to the organ-theft allegations that I was reporting.

As I told Evelyn about my story, her eyes went wide.

"Who would steal a heart valve from a *dead* person?" she asked. "And what would they do with it, anyway?"

"They probably sold it to a medical school someplace in exchange for some quick cash," I told her. "They're circling the wagons over at the ME's office, so it's hard to get access. And the police aren't talking to me right now at all, because I'm on the bottom of their shit list because of the story we ran about Antoine Hurley. They think I'm a traitor to the prosecution."

But I knew one guy who could find out what was going on over there.

I needed to put in a call to Fish.

The message light was blinking on the answering machine when I got home that night.

I hesitated before checking the message, wondering whether it might be Jonathan. He seldom called me on the landline, but leaving a message at home is just what I'd expect if he wanted to leave a message without danger of my picking up.

I could already feel the anger prickling in my fingertips as I punched in the numbers to retrieve the message. But the call was from Dr. Medina.

"Hi, Kate. I hope you don't mind me calling you at home," Medina's message began. "I just wanted to let you know that I really enjoyed our interview yesterday."

After a pause, he continued, "And hey. I was just wondering if you might like to have lunch or dinner with me this weekend, or whenever you're available. I don't know if you have a rule against dating the subjects of your stories, but I would really enjoy getting to know you better. I don't mind admitting that I'd like to see *you*." At the end of the message, he left his private cell number.

I wrote down the doctor's number. Then I replayed his message five more times, savoring each syllable of it.

I'd like to see you, his message had said.

Oh my God. Dr. Medina wants to go out with me. Medina must be attracted to me. To me.

No palpitating heart of a fifteen-year-old could have been launched farther into orbit by a guy's unexpected call. If a NASA space technician were to describe my emotions in strictly technical terms, he'd say I was jitterbugging on Jupiter.

I didn't even consider calling Medina back right away. That would come off as too eager. Let other women play the dating game according to modern rules by calling a guy back right away or even—no way!—calling him first. I preferred to wait. That was the way my mom had raised me, and she died before I got old enough to rebel.

Next I indulged in a completely adolescent girl-crush exercise. Sitting at my laptop in the dining room, I Googled Medina's name. I was looking for every tiny bit of information about him that existed out in cyberspace.

Most of the links that popped up were already familiar to me. I'd already researched Medina's background for my story about his thermal-laser-wand procedure, so it was hard to get anything new. But I did find a few interesting tidbits. Along with a handful of other doctors and medical personnel, he made yearly flights to Bolivia, Uruguay, and other impoverished parts of the globe to perform surgical operations for children. Medina specialized in correcting facial deformities in very young children. The charitable medical operation that he worked with was called Global Docs for Humanity. A news photo showed Medina posed against the backdrop of a mountaintop village, surrounded by children and smiling adults.

That's impressive, I thought.

From that point on, my fantasies took the brain helm; I was off and running to the Libido Races.

I tapped in a search for Titian's *Venus of Urbino*. My fingertips left faint sweatprints on the keyboard.

Articles and pictures of the famous reclining-nude painting flashed across the screen. I studied them for a while, absorbing some of the excerpts. Some reviewers of the painting conjectured: Was Titian's Venus a goddess? A courtesan? An archetype of the Renaissance Everywoman? This Venus had a look in her eyes of bold and uninhibited sexual desire. Her eyes dared the viewer to approach. She had one cheek nestled into her hair, which was a delicate cascade of reddish blond curls that spilled over her bared shoulder. After almost five hundred years, the Venus of Urbino remained an enigma. She was an object of desire for men for the ages.

The flushed feeling I'd first felt in Medina's office washed over me again.

Did Medina look at me like that? Did he see me the way Jonathan looked at Gi in the photo I'd seen of the two of them together? Jonathan had looked at Gi as if he'd wanted to rip her clothes off and do her, right in front of the camera. I *hated* the way Jonathan had looked at Gi.

Clearly I was overdue for a romantic sea change. I'd been focusing on Jonathan like he was Moby Dick, when there were tons of . . . ahem . . . *fish* in the sea.

Right at that moment, I gave myself a brand-new set of marching orders:

1. Stop whining about Jonathan.
2. Return Medina's phone call the next day.

I was washing my face in the bathroom when Elfie, who'd been rubbing against my ankles, suddenly froze. She shot out of the bathroom and dove under the bed.

Elfie is an excellent burglar alarm system. She responds the instant anyone sets foot outside the front door of my house.

Drying my face on a towel, I stepped into the bedroom. Then I paused to listen. It seemed quiet. Almost.

Through the living room, a faint sound was coming from the front door. It wasn't a knock exactly. It sounded like someone was slowly turning the doorknob. No sound could have been more chilling. Now *I* froze.

I certainly wasn't going to fling open the door to see who it was. Maybe it was simply someone disoriented or trying the wrong door. But that seemed unlikely.

As if to answer my question, the doorknob rattled back and forth. Violently this time. Someone shoved against the door. Trying to break in, and none too subtly.

I grabbed the wireless phone from its base by my bed. Sending up a prayer of thanks that a few months back I'd replaced the previous owner's flimsy locks with deadbolts, I punched in 911.

"This is Kate Gallagher," I said to the emergency operator who answered. "Someone is trying to break into my house right now. It's 221 Amber Lane. Please send a squad car as soon as possible. And please tell them to *hurry*."

Chapter 36

Dot Your Wand

Here's a little-known tip: Before you brush with your mascara wand, blot the end of the tip on a piece of tissue. That keeps the blobs from forming on your lashes.

—From The Little Book of Beauty Secrets by Mimi Morgan

It was time for a quick change of strategy.

The 911 operator had sent a squad car, but in the meantime I decided to become my own siren.

"I don't know who the hell you are, but the police are on the way!" I screamed toward the door.

Dashing into the kitchen, I grabbed a knife from the wooden knife block on the counter, and a skillet from the cupboard. Then I kicked the walls. Anything to make noise and scare who- ever it was off.

"Get *out* of here. Get *out*—get *out*!"

The 911 operator, who was still on the line,

said in a worried tone, "Miss Gallagher? What's happening? Are you okay?"

Bomp-bomp-bomp! Another sound at my front door. Only this was knocking, authoritative and official sounding. It couldn't be the intruder.

"Kate Gallagher?" a deep male voice said. "Durham Police Department."

Still clutching the skillet, knife, and phone in my hands, I crept to the door. I opened it a sliver. Two patrolmen stood there wearing serious-responder expressions. One of them I recognized from having covered previous crime scenes. I remembered his name was De la Cruz.

Letting the knife slip from my hand, I opened the door wider. (Never let a cop see a knife in your hand under any circumstances, by the way. It can be dangerous.)

"You got here really fast," I said to De la Cruz.

"One of your neighbors called—you got a great neighborhood watch here. What happened, Miss Gallagher?" De la Cruz said to me. The fact that he didn't need to confirm who I was meant that he'd obviously recognized me, too.

I explained the twisty doorknob sound to them, plus the pushing-on-the-door thing that had scared the bejesus out of me. I have to admit, my explanation sounded much less dramatic than the experience had *felt* in real time.

"So you didn't get a look at the guy?" De la Cruz said, while making some notes in his report pad.

"No," I said. "I just made as much noise as I could to scare him off."

The other cop, who'd been examining the doorknob, straightened up. "Hey, Cruz," he said. "Take a look. I found jimmy marks."

"Jimmy marks?" I said. "Are those from the guy trying to break in?"

"Yup. Definitely," De la Cruz said, peering at the brass doorknob. "It was probably an attempted burglary. We've had a bunch of them around here lately. Usually they take place during the daytime when no one's home, though. Not at night. It sounds like they came here looking for trouble."

Looking for trouble. I thought about Anaïs Loring of the Newbodies, and how she'd been murdered during a home-invasion robbery. At *night*.

The chill I'd felt earlier washed over me again. I checked my watch. It was nearly ten thirty. I'd heard the first sound of the intruder around ten.

It's like evil karma is stalking the Newbodies, Evelyn had said to me the other night on the phone. *Who's next?*

Was it supposed to have been *me*?

Chapter 37

Waist-Cincher Magic

If you haven't discovered waist cinchers yet, run, do not walk, to the undergarment section of your department store. These miracle support garments suck your waist in by several inches. Oh my God. I never leave home without one, especially when I'm feeling bloated.

—From *The Little Book of Beauty Secrets* by Mimi Morgan

Fish kept vigil on my couch into the wee hours of Thursday morning, just to make sure I was safe. I think he was secretly hoping my intruder would return, just so he could kick some intruder ass.

In addition to appointing himself my personal watchdog, Fish had promised to follow up with the medical examiner's office to find out who had illegally sold Jana's heart valve.

"I know a guy who knows a guy over in the ME's office," Fish said. "And my guy owes me money. I'll call in a favor."

"That's fabulous," I said.

Then I mentioned my weird encounter with
Chaz Putnam to Fish.

"There was something wrong in the way he
freaked out about Jana's purse," I told him. "I
know the kid's a dopehead and he didn't want
the cops coming over, but his response was way
over the top. He practically broke my wrist. Can
you check him out?"

"Sure thing. He sounds like a punk."

Fish had left by the time a package arrived on
the porch for me Thursday morning. Carefully
wrapped in brown paper and twine, the box was
small but surprisingly heavy, as if it contained
metal ball bearings. Or maybe electronics. It was
from my dad.

A neon red label on the outside said:

CAUTION
DANGER OF ELECTRICAL SHOCK IF PACKAGE IS
OPENED BY UNAUTHORIZED PERSONNEL
HANDLE WITH EXTREME CARE
CONTAINS EMD TECHNOLOGY COMPONENTS

Next to that sobering warning, another sticker
depicted a jagged bolt of electricity.

What in the world? I wondered as I carried the
box inside and set it on the kitchen counter.

I dug through my memory, trying to recall what my dad had said earlier this week about what he was sending to me. Something about a radio, I seemed to recall. Or maybe some kind of solar appliance. An earthquake kit—that was it.

Using my pocketknife, I cut through the cord.

Inside the box, a note lay on top of a layer of Styrofoam peanuts:

> *Kate,*
> *The enclosed device is legal in your state, so don't worry. It's not lethal, but you'll find that it is a very effective defense against any assailant. You'll need to practice a bit to get the hang of this type of weapon. I've sent you the model that's used by police and the military. Please be sure to carry it with you at all times.*
> *And be careful out there!*
> *Love, Dad*

Underneath the peanuts was a smaller box with the label ELECTRO-MUSCULAR DISRUPTION DEVICE. Inside was a strange, futuristic-looking gun. Not a firearm—it was a Taser weapon, better known as a stun gun.

It was covered in a black-and-white zebra-striped pattern.

Obviously this must be the women's model, I

thought, turning it over gingerly in my hands.
Unless maybe the stripes were supposed to con-
fuse predators in tall savannah grass.

The gun came with an instructional DVD. I
popped it into my laptop and watched it intently.

Instead of a long barrel, the firing end of the
stun gun was a bulky black box. When you
wanted to fire the weapon, you released a safety
latch. Then a laser beam enabled you to aim exactly where you wanted to fire a pair of electric
probes. The probes delivered a jolt of fifteen
joules of electricity—enough to incapacitate an
attacker and leave him dazed but cause no permanent damage.

The optimal range for firing was seven feet.
The probes—barblike metal prongs attached to
wires—would deliver a stunning jolt to an assailant. The electric charge was supposed to work
through clothing. The police version that my dad
had sent me was stronger than the typical con-
sumer version—supposedly it would work even
through body armor. My dad had thoughtfully
included two leather holsters—one for wearing
underclothing, the other for attaching inside a
purse.

Wow.

Never before had I been willing to carry any
kind of gun. The idea of toting a firearm had always been anathema to me. My father and I had

spent endless family meals arguing over the subject.

But times changed. The encounter with the intruder the night before had just succeeded where years of arguments from my dad had failed.

Standing now in front of my bathroom mirror, I assumed a shooting stance.

"You talkin' to *me*?" I did my best Travis Bickle pose from *Taxi Driver*, taking aim at an imaginary assailant.

Then I lowered it. The idea of toting around a Tom-Swiftian electric popgun for personal protection seemed bizarre in the extreme. Especially when the gun in question looked like a zebra-striped water pistol. Any assailant worth his bad-guy chops would probably bust out laughing at sight of the thing.

That would lower an assailant's guard and give you an advantage in a fight, the little voice in my head said.

I shoved the stun gun in the leather holster and snapped it onto my purse.

It slid right in.

Chapter 38

Fake Advantage

Here's a bit of trickery. When you're applying fake lashes, use black glue for the lashes, not clear. The black glue will blend in and look like eyeliner.

—From *The Little Book of Beauty Secrets* by Mimi Morgan

"Has anyone ever told you that you're incredibly beautiful, Kate?"

"Incredibly beautiful? Let's see. Yes. A guy at a bar said that to me once—right before he passed out."

"I'm serious." Medina smiled at me from the other end of the canoe we were paddling.

"I'm serious, too. The bouncers had to drag him out of the bar by his ankles."

Medina and I were making our way across Harmony Pond, a charming urban oasis tucked at the edge of Durham. A rattan picnic box rested on the floor of the canoe between us, waiting to be unpacked. This was our first date, and I was so nervous I was ready to jump ship.

"Why does my saying you're beautiful embarrass you so much?" Medina continued. "I'm sure men must tell you that all the time."

I'm sure they didn't. But what was more embarrassing at that moment was that I'd just felt my end of the canoe scrape bottom. How unharmonius. If we ran aground and had to portage our way back to the docks, I'd be so humiliated, I'd have to drown myself in the pond scum.

We finally made it to a small man-made island and disembarked. The center of the island featured a set of rounded granite steps. At the top of the steps sat a small-scale replica of a Greek temple.

Medina looked up at the temple, then at me. "Okay, so maybe the temple's a little hokey, but what incredible light. Wouldn't the French Impressionists have loved this spot? And they would have loved to paint you standing in it, I might add."

"I can see Seurat doing that temple in that wonderful pointillism style of his. A bucolic urban island."

"All we'd need is a parasol for you and a top hat for me."

"And Seurat. We'd need him, of course."

Medina gave me a delighted grin. "So now that I know you like art, I have to try to trip you up," he said. "Let's go a little further back in time."

Pointing up the stairs at the temple, he said, "Are those Ionic, Corinthian, or Doric columns up there on our Greek temple?"

I studied them for a moment. "They're none of the above, Professor Pop Quiz," I finally said. "They're Chirons—a mixture of those styles. The temple's architect put a proverbial man's head on a horse's body."

"Where'd you learn all that? In college?"

"Wellesley. There's still some value in a liberal arts education, no matter what those MIT frat boys say. Where'd you study art?"

"Oh, I've been a lifelong appreciator of everything aesthetic," he said, letting his gaze linger on my face. "Especially the human aesthetic."

"Is that how you wound up going into plastic surgery?"

"I got my start in middle school," he said. "Helping my older sister do her makeup for dates. I believe my mom thought I was gay until I started hitting on my sister's girlfriends."

"How'd you make out with the older-woman crowd, if you don't mind my asking?"

"I love your asking, in fact. I did fantastic."

Flexing his fingers he said, "I developed this

insane neck-rub technique. If you don't mind a professional brag, by age twelve my neck rubs were far superior to anything you can get in some chiroquack's office. I practiced on our dog until I got it down pat. My sister's friends loved my neck jobs so much, they used to pay me fifty cents for five minutes. That's where I first started training the muscles in my surgeon's fingers, by putting the moves on the girls of Morris Township, New Jersey."

While I was still taking that in, he added, "So I'd like your professional opinion, Kate. Do you think any of those girls I neck-rubbed for cash will bust me for my past as a junior high gigolo? I'm afraid of winding up on *Entertainment Tonight*."

"Okay, *ding-ding-ding*! That's my bullshit meter going off," I said. "You totally made up that whole story about the dog and the fingers and the girls' necks."

"Would these fingers lie to you?"

Facing the temple on the hill, Medina placed a hand over his heart. "As Zeus is my witness," he said. "Absolutely true. Except for the dog part."

"Hmm. Well, as Scarlett O'Hara said, 'As God is my witness, I'll never be hungry again.' I'm hungry, so can we eat our picnic now?"

"I thought you'd never ask. And don't worry—I didn't bring any radishes with me, Miss Scarlett."

It was much too soon for my heart to fall for someone new, but my taste buds rolled over for Medina's gourmet picnic faster than a cheap date on Hollywood Boulevard.

He unpacked an astonishing array of treats from the woven basket he'd brought in the canoe. When the unwrapping revealed nuggets of roasted portabella mushroom, goat cheese, and red peppers on focaccia, I broke into applause.

"Now I can't wait to see the dessert," I said.

"Oh, that will be the best of all," he replied. "I made chocolate *pot de crème* with fresh raspberries. My grandmother's recipe."

If Medina had summoned Zeus from the temple above us and asked him to pronounce us man and wife at that very moment, my stomach would have happily said *I do*.

Over the chocolate and glasses of dry rosé, our conversation turned much more serious. I finally told Medina that his patient Jana had been my friend.

"I didn't know you knew her. That carjacking was such a horrible tragedy," he said. "My heart went out to her family. In fact, she had an appointment with me the afternoon before it happened."

"I know. I had lunch with her that day, by coincidence. She'd just come from the appointment at your office."

Medina's eyebrows shot up. "Wow, that *is* a coincidence," he said. "You don't by any chance have a camera crew hiding behind the temple ready to ambush me with questions about my patient, do you? I know you're a good reporter but . . ."

"No, silly!" I laughed, a bit too hard.

When my laughter died away, a jolt of sadness replaced it. "Actually, all I know about Jana's death right now is a bunch of disconnected information," I said. "The police seem to be in a hurry to put her case behind them. They've arrested the guy they say shot her. They don't seem to want to know about anything that doesn't fit in with their story line."

"I know. I saw that piece you did on the news. His name is Antoine something?"

"Antoine Hurley. But I can't let it go at what they're saying. There's something missing for me in the picture they're trying to paint. Maybe there's too much noise on the graph, as my old science teacher would say."

Medina plucked a long blade of grass. "Well, you know what the artist Seurat would do in this situation."

"No. What would he do?"

Turning the blade of grass on its side like a scalpel, he traced a line around my lips. "Seurat believed that you have to juxtapose all the tiny, disconnected dots of color next to one another," he said. "Then you have to take a step back to see the big picture. That's the only way you'll see what's really going on in the painting.

"So you have to put all the color dots—those are all your disconnected bits of data—down on the canvas. Then take a step back. That's when you'll be able to see what shapes emerge."

Medina kept stroking my skin with the blade of grass. Long, slow brushstrokes. The sensation gave me goose bumps. I felt hypnotized.

I don't know diddly-squat about colored dots, but that grass-blade thing gave me the most sensual feeling I'd had in months. And we hadn't even kissed yet.

That came next.

When I got back to the studio from our lunchtime picnic, I decided to test out Medina's theory about brainstorming by using color-point analysis. Maybe art theory could actually help me think through Jana's murder.

Put all the color-dots—those are your disconnected bits of data—down on the canvas, he'd said. *Then take a step back. That's when you'll be able to see what shapes emerge.*

Of course you could write that same information down and then start brainstorming, but I liked the idea of taking a more visual approach to brainstorming. The problem was that my artistic skills stopped developing when I was in kindergarten. So when I got back to the studio I decided to use technology to substitute for talent. I'm sure Seurat would have approved. In fact, I'm sure he would have been a computer genius on top of all his other abilities.

Using a shareware program I downloaded from the Web, I assigned a specific color to every type of information I could think of that was related to Jana's murder. The information bits, colored by type, appeared as small bubbles. Then I told the program to sort the bubbles in various ways. I kept adding and sorting the information bits, looking for patterns.

An hour later, all I could see in the dots was a kaleidoscopic bubble bath.

What I did *not* see, interestingly, were very many green bubbles, which was the color assigned to the police's favorite suspect, Antoine Hurley.

Most of the bubbles were in the yellow zone. That was surprising. Yellow was the color I'd assigned to the information about the Putnams' house and Jana's purse. It was as if the clustering of the bubbles indicated that there was some importance to the fact that Jana had left her purse at the Putnams' house on the night of the Newbodies get-together.

My graph didn't jibe with what Luke and the other homicide investigators were saying. Maybe my bubble theory was for the birds.

I pinned the graph on the side of my cubicle and sat for a while, staring at it. I definitely felt that the exercise had been worthwhile. The bubbles were definitely showing me something. But I couldn't get ahold of the image.

Clearly I'd need a genius like Seurat to figure this whole thing out.

I realized I hadn't spoken to Shaina since her uncle Belmont had whisked her away to the Bahamas.

I called the cell phone number she'd given me.

Shaina picked up right away and said she was doing great.

"I'm coming back to Durham next week," she said. "I want to talk to the police again. I feel bad."

"About what?"

"I was so upset when I first talked to them about the carjacking. I just don't think that guy who took the car shot Mom. I think there was someone else involved. Maybe someone who was waiting around the corner for them."

Chapter 39

Stocking Talk

Lots of women these days don't like to wear nylons. I totally don't get this. (P.S. Wearing shoes without nylons makes your feet smell.) Stockings even out your skin tone and don't have to be uncomfortable.

—From *The Little Book of Beauty Secrets* by Mimi Morgan

"I've found out that the human-organ racket is fishier than my last name," Fish said.

"You mean it's fishier than this crab cake? This dish tastes like last week's haul from China."

"I told you to order the steak burger. It's the only thing here that's decent, other than the booze, that is."

I was pretending to nibble the early-bird plate at Fish's favorite hangout, a sports bar named Hail Mary's.

Fish was finishing up his second drink of the day even though it was only four o'clock. To keep up with him I ordered another club soda with

lime, much to the amusement of our plump-
armed waitress.

"I know there are some bad operators out
there who get illegal body parts," I said to Fish
across the table of our padded booth, "but you
make the entire human-organ business sound
criminal, like sex trafficking. Don't forget about
all the people who are waiting for kidneys and
hearts. I mean, some people *die* before they get a
transplant. What about them?"

"Those people are the ten percent of the
iceberg that's above the waterline. Underneath,
you have scumbags out there stealing body
parts, paying broke people for kidneys. And
even worse."

"So please enlighten me, Fish. Exactly which
part of this racket is related to what happened to
Jana Miller's body?"

"Here's your answer." He slid a manila folder
across the polished wood table.

I opened the file and scanned its contents. The
folder was filled with pages of blurry printouts.
They appeared to be copies of the fronts and
backs of bank checks.

"Okay, I'm looking at a bunch of checks that
were made out to some guy named Sateesh
Kumar," I said, trying to make sense of it. All the
checks were written for large amounts.

Fish tapped his fingertips on the papers, leaving wet fingerprints. "Look at the—"

"Hey, don't get these copies of the checks wet." I snatched away the papers. "In case I need to get cut shots of these later for a story."

Wiping off his hands on a crummy napkin, Fish said, "This guy Sateesh travels overseas a lot. He's hooked into a ring of thugs that kidnaps children. These kidnappers hold them in poverty-stricken places like the Ivory Coast and parts of South America."

"Why?"

"Why do you think? For their organs."

"Whoa. Wait a second, Fish," I countered. "I've heard of people stealing human organs from dead bodies, but you're talking about living human beings. About *children*, for God's sake. Stop it."

Fish knocked back the last of his drink. "You're a reporter, aren't you? Don't be so fucking naive, Kate," he said. "Some of these children are being held—alive—for their body parts."

"They take the organs . . . the kidneys, you mean? Surgically?"

"I suspect it's even worse than anyone knows. These animals could easily be killing the children, once they have them under their control. Even if they stay alive, they're put into the sex-trafficking business.

"We're talking about body snatchers, Kate," he

said. "Modern-day, walking vampires—they don't value human life at all."

The thought of children being kidnapped—being *harvested*—for their bodies and organs made me literally sick to my stomach. I shoved my crab plate aside.

"Why do you think Sateesh Kumar is involved in something horrible like this?" I asked, staring across the table at Fish.

"His rap sheet, for one thing," he replied. "Interpol has a big file on Sateesh. I heard he's been holed up around here someplace. Shacked up with a hot-looking babe."

"Bull*shit*, Fish."

"What? You mean you've heard she's not hot?"

"No. I mean if you and the cops know so much about Sateesh, why's he free to walk around Durham?"

"Maybe they haven't caught up with him yet," he said.

"Well, I'm not buying this yet."

The waitress appeared at our table again.

"Another club soda for you, miss?" she asked me.

"Actually, I think I'll take a whiskey sour this time."

The waitress nodded knowingly. "Sure thing," she said. "Everyone goes for the booze after talking to this pier rat long enough. Right, Fish?"

"Right, Pris," he said, rattling his ice cubes at her. "And you know me . . ."

"Got it. Another hard one on the rocks."

"Yup."

As Pris returned to the bar, I considered the checks in my hand. "But even if your information about Sateesh is correct, what could be the connection between Jana's murder and her heart valve being stolen, I'm wondering?"

"Probably none," Fish replied. "The stolen valve was just one of life's weird coincidences. Jana's body turned up in County Morgue at the wrong place, wrong time. But at least this crime we can track."

Jana's death seemed to be riddled with weird coincidences. That's exactly what Luke had said about Anaïs Loring of the Newbodies being murdered six months before Jana—just a coincidence. Another dot of color on the canvas.

Fish, who'd been watching me think, added impatiently, "Take a look at some of these parties who wrote checks to Sateesh. That'll give you a good idea of who's supporting this scumbag."

"New Wave Technologies," I read the name slowly out loud. "Prana Centers. Dr. . . ."

With unsteady fingers, I picked up the printout of the check to study it more closely. There was no mistake.

"What are you looking at?" Fish asked.

"Hang on a second."

That second was all the time it took for my heart to fall to the floor of my chest. On its way south it collided with an upsurge of bile, which flooded my mouth with a rancid taste of crab.

Written in flowing black ink, the signature at the bottom of the check read:

Dr. Xavier Medina

Chapter 40

Your Nighttime Skin Routine—It's Good for the Skin, Good for the Brain!

Washing your skin at bedtime is important on many levels. It removes impurities from your skin, and it also serves as a signal to your brain that it's time to relax. This helps you wind down and release the stress from your day.

—From *The Little Book of Beauty Secrets* by Mimi Morgan

The address on the upper-left portion of the check was that of Medina's office in Durham. There was no mistake. It was my Medina.

"This check," I said. "It's signed by someone I know. Dr. Xavier Medina."

"Who's he?

"A local plastic surgeon. A very well-known guy. He does charity work with children in Africa and South America," I said.

"Oh, yeah?" Fish snorted into his drink. "I'll just bet he does. Does he steal their livers, too?"

I noted the check number and date. Three

months earlier, Medina had written a check to Sateesh Kumar for $999. If what Fish was saying about Sateesh Kumar was correct—that the man was a "modern-day vampire" who plied his trade in illegal human organs—then Medina might be involved with a criminal.

Leaning back from the table, I said, "It's hard for me to believe that your information about Sateesh Kumar is true, Fish. In fact, I *don't* believe it. Xavier has a wonderful reputation. He can't be involved with anyone like that."

"Oh, it's *Xavier*, is it?"

Grabbing the check from me, Fish made an elaborate show of examining it, then said, "Tell me the truth, Kate. Are you sweet on this guy? Because you sound like someone who's fucking someone."

"Certainly I'm not," I said, as the tips of my ears began to burn. "I'm just saying—what if your information about Sateesh is wrong?"

"And what if it's right? Your honey-doc could be doing business with a world-class criminal."

"I'm going to find out," I said. "Right now."

I reached under the table for my laptop. I was pleased to discover that Hail Mary's had free Wi-Fi. I did a quick search for several Sateesh Kumars, cross-referencing the names with information from Fish's file.

I looked at him. "According to what I've just found," I said, "the Sateesh Kumar who has an Interpol record has been sitting in prison in Chad for the last five years. And *this* check that was written by Xavier Medina was drafted two months ago. To a local Sateesh. On a local bank. So it can't possibly be the same Sateesh Kumar, right?"

Fish stared at the check for a long moment, then shrugged. "Maybe."

"*Maybe*, my ass. And for your information, Mr. Potato Head, Sateesh and Kumar are both common names in India. There are probably a half million guys walking around with that same name."

"Hey, I didn't beat up anyone, did I?" Smiling, Fish lifted his drink in a peace toast. "We're just doing a little partner research here."

"Hmmph."

"And speaking of research," he said, ignoring the fact that I was continuing to fume, "Remember you asked me a while back to look into a rich stoner kid? The Putnam kid?"

"Chaz? Yeah—what about him?"

"Well I just got a callback from a pal at a credit agency. After I called to ask him about Chaz, he discovered that the kid is running a one-man server farm for fraudulent credit cards. My friend has already called the authorities to get him shut down. It'll take some time, though."

"What's a server farm? And does it have anything to do with Jana?"

"Sure it does. Server farms are groups of computers that relay stolen credit information to other users. Chaz got a hold of Jana's credit card numbers—and evidently tried to run them."

"That makes sense," I said. "Chaz told me he had computers in his room that he didn't want the police to see, although I didn't connect it with Jana's death at the time. He must've gotten the cards from Jana's purse. She left it behind at Trish Putnam's house the night of the Newbodies meeting."

"The thing is, according to my pal, Jana had already closed the credit cards by the time the Chaz kid got a hold of the card numbers. My guess is Jana had shut them down to cut off the money tree to that low-life husband she was about to divorce, Gavin Spellmore."

"That's right. She told me about that."

"And here's where it gets *real* interesting. I guess when Chaz couldn't wring any dough out of Jana's cards, he got royally pissed. According to another buddy of mine at the phone company, he placed a cell phone call to one Akito Carver.

That last bit's on the QT, by the way—it's totally illegal for my phone buddy to have given me that information."

"Akito Carver?" I said. "I heard about him from Antoine Hurley's defense attorney. Akito goes by the street name Mad Dog."

"Right, and word all over the street is that Mad Dog is Chaz's drug dealer," Fish said. "I can't believe those broke-dicks over at homicide missed that fact."

I leaned forward in excitement. "I reported that Mad Dog may have been the guy who actually shot Jana," I said. "And he's also Chaz's drug dealer? And Chaz phoned him on the night of Jana's murder?"

When Fish nodded, I added, "Maybe Chaz told Mad Dog to steal Jana's car that night and it got ugly," I said. "It became a carjacking and murder."

"So that would mean that little ol' Chaz Putnam lit the fuse on Mad Dog, who went out and murdered Jana," Fish said. "While Chaz never even got his hands dirty."

I sat bolt upright. Another surge ran through my body—this one of alarm.

"Uh-oh," I said. "Evelyn's evil karma."

"What karma?" Fish stared at me. "Are you going California frosted flaky on me?"

"I'm remembering how Anaïs Loring was killed in a home-invasion robbery," I said. "And the attempted break-in at *my* house. What if Chaz was behind those incidents? What if he's targeting the women in his mom's Newbodies group for their credit cards, and using Mad Dog as the muscle? If that's true, everyone in the group is in danger."

Chapter 41

Don't Skip the Yearly Skin Checkup

Have your dermatologist check your skin once a year. You need to keep on top of sun damage. Sun exposure that you had when you were twelve years old can come back to haunt you when you're fifty.

—From *The Little Book of Beauty Secrets* by Mimi Morgan

Fish left the bar to try to get in touch with his former colleagues at the Durham PD to tell them about Chaz Putnam and the link to Jana's carjacking. I wasn't too sure they'd put much stock in information from "a drunk and a psych case."

So I started making some calls, too.

First I left a message on Luke's cell phone. But because my own reputation with Luke was in the deep freeze, I didn't expect to get much response from the homicide detective.

Then I called Evelyn.

"Where are you right now?" I asked when she picked up. I could hear women talking in the background.

"I'm at Trish's house," she said. "A few of us are having a board meeting to follow up on—"

"You're at Trish *Putnam's* house? Where's her son, Chaz?"

"Um, I don't know," she said. "He's upstairs in his room, I guess. Want me to have Trish go find him?"

"*No!*" Jesus. I might have actually made things worse by calling. If Chaz had anything to do with Jana's carjacking, making him suspicious might put Evelyn and the other women in danger. Especially if Mad Dog was nearby.

"Look, Evelyn, forget that I called, okay?" I said. "Don't tell Trish anything. Don't even tell her that I called just now. And if you see Chaz, don't tell him anything about *anything*. You understand?"

"You sound weird, Kate," Evelyn said with a giggle. "Have we been sipping some bubbly?"

"Don't say my name again. Please, Evelyn— I'm incredibly serious. Just hang up."

"Okay." She clicked off.

If there'd been wings bolted to the sides of my Z4, I would have gone airborne. That's how fast I drove from Hail Mary's bar to Trish's house.

I was hoping to get stopped for speeding. But of course, there's never a cop around when you really *want* one.

I wasn't sure that it was a good idea to show up at Trish's house. I simply had an overwhelming sense that the recent events were coming to a crisis point, and I wanted to move my friends out of harm's way.

When I arrived at Trish's colonial house, the porch lights were blazing. Several cars were parked at the curb. I recognized Evelyn's pink Mini Cooper.

When I rang the doorbell, Trish answered and gave me a surprised smile.

"I didn't know you could make it tonight, Kate—come on in," she said. "We're just finishing up some board business, but you're welcome to join us."

Taking a deep breath, I followed Trish into the living room.

Monique, Celia, Evelyn, and several other women were sprawled out on Trish's pasha pillows.

"Actually, I'm sorry to bust in like this, but I heard a report at the studio," I announced. "There's been a gas leak in the neighborhood. You should all move to another location," I said.

"*What*?" Trish's eyes went extraround. "Oh, my gosh. Let me go find Chaz."

"Uh, wait a second, Trish—"

As soon as Trish disappeared, I faced the other women.

"You guys—I want you to get out of this house. *Right now.* Quietly. Please. I don't have time to explain, but I think Chaz was behind Jana's carjacking. Stay together and don't be by yourself tonight. There was someone else involved, and he's really dangerous."

Everyone made shocked-sounding murmurs, but they started moving.

Except for Evelyn. She remained on her pasha pillow, staring at me.

"Are you *sure* about this, Kate?" she said.

"Yes, Kate," a male voice said. "Are you *sure*?"

I spun around.

Chaz was standing behind me.

I backed off. As I moved, I reached into my purse and extracted the stun gun. Just in case I needed it.

"Kate?" Trish appeared next to Chaz. She had a carry-on bag slung over her shoulder.

With a confused-looking expression on her face, she said, "Aren't we leaving? What about the gas leak?"

"Trish, there actually isn't a gas leak," I said. "I came here to tell you some bad news about what Chaz has been up to."

Turning to Chaz, I said, "Why don't you tell your mother about Mad Dog and your server farm and your pot deals. Then we'll talk about Jana's carjacking."

Trish glared at Chaz. *"Pot?"* she said. "You have marijuana in your room?"

As Chaz rolled his eyes, I heard a banging sound. It was coming from French doors that opened off one side of the living room.

A moment later the doors gave way. A tall, heavily built African-American male stepped into the room. I recognized him instantly from the picture that I'd seen at Violet Hurley's house.

It was Mad Dog.

He was holding an AK-47 in his hands.

Chapter 42

How to Lose Weight Without Exercising

Good news! You don't have to exercise to stay skinny. Studies have shown that chronic fidgeters burn off enough calories to stay slim.

—From *The Little Book of Beauty Secrets* by Mimi Morgan

The moment I saw Mad Dog and the huge gun, everything downshifted into slow motion. I knew in my gut that he'd burst into Trish's house to spray the room with bullets. He meant to kill everyone inside.

Seven feet. Optimal distance. The DVD instructions for the stun gun replayed through my head as if I were watching them. All I could do was see Mad Dog and his gun and calculate what I needed to do. The Taser in my hand. Seven feet away from the target.

I stepped toward Mad Dog . . . released the safety latch.

Bullets from Mad Dog's semiautomatic gun

began tearing into Trish's walls. There were sounds of glass breaking. Evelyn screaming.

I aimed the red laser dots at the middle of Mad Dog's chest. I remember he was wearing a white T-shirt that had a green can of beer on it.

For one split second, Mad Dog seemed to pause as he registered the zebra stripes on my stun gun. I thought I saw his lips curl.

That's when I fired.

The probes went zinging into the beer can on Mad Dog's T. He let out a grunt of pain, then doubled over and collapsed.

Mad Dog writhed around on the rug, like the dog that got French-fried at Pompeii.

I kicked away the AK-47. Then I picked it up, just to make sure that Chaz didn't get any sudden bright ideas.

Miraculously, no one had been hit. Evelyn and Trish had pounced on Mad Dog. They were pounding him on the head. Chaz was crouched behind the settee. Coward.

I could see a flicker of blue lights. They were strobing in from somewhere outside. It was a rescue posse.

"So how did the cops know to come to that house last night?"

It was the next night. Medina was all ears as I

recounted my encounter with Mad Dog at Trish's house.

We were sitting next to each other on my couch with the television tuned to channel twelve, waiting to watch the first installment of my weight-loss series. After that we were planning to celebrate by going someplace incredibly fattening for dinner. Medina had just finished meeting Elfie for the first time. And I think the introduction had gone pretty well. Elfie had extended her paw to him, which in cat body language means *you're in*.

"It was the homicide cops who showed up at the house," I said. "Fish and I had both left messages about Chaz Putnam for them. They came over to question him, right at the moment that Mad Dog Carver decided to take care of his 'exposure' on Jana's murder and the robbery scheme by killing Chaz, and anyone else who happened to be there."

"So this Mad Dog character and the Chaz kid were in cahoots?"

"Yes, but Chaz wasn't counting on the murders. When that started, evidently he tried to get out, but Mad Dog wouldn't let him. He shot Jana, and before that Anaïs Loring, the cops told me last night. And I'm sure we'll find out that he was the one who tried to break into my place."

"Wow. Your life is so exciting," Medina said. "I

just hope I can keep up. But what ever happened to Jana's autopsy results? You told me that her heart valve had been stolen by someone. Have they found out who did it?"

"There's your answer," I said, pointing at the television. Channel Twelve News was showing a technician being escorted into the county jail.

"The detectives had the wrong killer in Jana's case, but at least they tracked down the sleaze-bag who tried to sell her heart valve," I said. "For a while, I even mistakenly thought *you* might have been involved with that."

"Me?"

I told Medina that Fish had turned up a check made out to Sateesh Kumar, signed by Medina.

"There's a Sateesh Kumar who is an international organ smuggler, but I realized it couldn't be the same guy you wrote the check to," I said. "Who is the Sateesh you wrote the check to, by the way?"

"My periodontist. He's a heck of a nice guy, by the way. Does excellent root canals."

"Sateesh Kumar is your *periodontist*? That's too funny."

Glancing at the TV again, I added, "Oops, my weight-loss story is coming on now. I'm not sure I want to watch this."

"Well, *I* do."

The first installment of my fat-scam series

flashed across the screen. I tensed for Medina's reaction to the "money shot" of my torso in a bikini being shrink-wrapped by Yolanda the Russian. But then I remembered that he'd already seen me naked during the laser treatment and still was attracted to me. So there you had it.

Medina looked from the screen to me on the couch. "I don't know why you were so nervous about this story," he said. "You look amazing."

Reaching into his pocket, he said, "Here, I want to show you something."

He handed me a white cardboard envelope. Inside was a souvenir photograph. It showed Medina and me in the canoe at Harmony Pond.

I was smiling up at the camera. But in the photo Medina was looking at me. He had an expression in his eyes that I absolutely loved. He was looking at me like he wanted to rip all my clothes off and do me right then and there. Right in front of the ducks.

"Is it okay if I hang on to this photograph?" I asked him.

"Of course," he replied. "We're going to have lots more like these. With any luck, we'll have albums."

Oh, yes.

About the Author

Kathryn Lilley is a former television journalist and a lifelong dieter. She lives in Southern California. Visit her on the Web at www.kathrynlilley.com.